STARFADE

A Realm Blender
Novella

GARY SWABY

STARFADE

Copyright © 2019 by Gary Swaby.

For information contact :
Redital Publishing
www.reditalgroup.com/publishing
www.garyaswaby.com

Book and cover design by Redital Publishing

ISBN: 978-1-9160066-3-8

First Edition: March 2019.

CHAPTER ONE

FROM THE GROUND, the communications tower showed no signs of being tampered with by wildlife. "Interesting," said Chiaki, to herself. "We must have unwanted visitors." Originally, she thought that maybe the winds had disrupted the tower, although they hadn't been so fierce today. It was clear now that someone had come within the planet's atmosphere. Chiaki wondered how her alerts hadn't triggered the moment another ship came within range of the satellite.

She wasn't able to make contact with her friends at the base with the communications tower being down, nor could she try to make contact with her unwanted guest. But she didn't pride herself on being the most gifted hacker in the Milky Way for no reason.

She weighed her options as she peered up the tower. She could climb up, but that would take too long. She wanted to get back to her video game as soon as possible. She'd been in the middle of a competitive online match, and now her team would lose because of her abrupt departure from the game.

Luckily for her, she had created a private network with a limited range. She had a few nifty tools connected to this network.

"Tobi," she called, summoning her A.I assistant. She stared at her Comm-link device, strapped to her left forearm. Blue sound waves rippled on the screen.

"I'm here, Nova, but I cannot connect to the network."

"Yes, I know that," she said. "Please, use the local network to summon the Skylifter." Chiaki watched the blue swirl on her Comm-link as Tobi registered the command.

"It's on its way now," said Tobi, in its British accent.

"Xièxiè." she smiled.

"Chinese today? You haven't practiced your Japanese for some time," said Tobi.

"Hey, just because I'm half and half, it doesn't mean I need to speak both." The truth was that she only held onto the Chinese word of gratitude because it was the last thing she'd heard her brother say.

She could hear the Skylifter wheeling itself towards her now; its wheels bumping on the rocky paths of Flade. Each bump making it sway to the point it could tip over. Flade was a small planet that her brother had been given by a client who could not pay him for a job. Chiaki had inherited the planet from her brother after his murder.

"The Skylifter has arrived, Nova," said Tobi.

"Thanks again, now go enjoy the peace of being disconnected."

Chiaki climbed the ladder attached to the side of the Skylifter and swung her legs over the edge, one by one. She held the joysticks and drove it towards the tower. "Tobi, I know you don't have access to all your data right now; but do you have anything in your cached memory that would give you an idea which asshole would come knocking on my door today?"

"Nothing," said Tobi. "Currently, I only have a record of your last job on Mars. You successfully retrieved all recorded data on Ernest Gorbitson's great-grandmother."

"Well, Mars is full of assholes. Maybe I pissed someone off," she said, as she set the Skylifter to rise. Chiaki knew that probably wasn't the case. She'd programmed Flade's security so well that no average being could show up without triggering her alerts. She knew that whoever was out there must have access to some serious tech.

She thought of her brother Kura's murder. He'd had no planetwide security systems in place that day. Only the hideout itself had been secured. Meaning, he'd let his murderer through the doors. It must have been a client of his. All she needed was some evidence, and she'd murder them herself. She'd been through all of his records and she'd investigated all known clients, but she suspected that the one who'd taken Kura from her had been undocumented.

When the Skylifter had extended as high as it could go, she grabbed a rope that she kept inside for occasions like these. She wasn't scared of heights, but she liked precautions. It was what made her such a reliable hacker.

Just as she clamped her hand on the cold space-metal of the tower, she heard the unmistakable sound of a shuttle car descending through the sky. "Shit!" she said, running to peek over the opposite side of the Skylifter.

A white shuttle was landing below. "Call, incoming," said Tobi.

"Keep it ringing, Tobi," she said. "I'm going to try and find out who it is first." Chiaki loaded up the touchscreen keypad on her Comm-link and keyed in a number of commands to obtain the callers' Comm-ID while the call was pending. "Almost got it," she said, observing the first set of three numbers as they loaded one by one in a sequence.

Before the ID finished displaying, the call was dropped. Through her peripheral vision, she saw the shuttle's doors open up. A pair of armored feet revealed themselves from the gap. Soon enough, Chiaki was looking at a Galactic Alliance marine with blond curls, clutching a megaphone.

I should have known, she thought.

"This is Commander Pearson of the Galactic Alliance. We have infiltrated your hideout; please come down. We will not take action if you co-operate."

Chiaki hurled saliva over the side of the Skylifter.

CHAPTER TWO

ALLIANCE MARINE OR NOT, Chiaki would not stand for people trespassing on her planet. Her irritation led her to raise her SMG at the marine as soon as she touched the ground. She didn't care that he was equipped with a rifle that could drop her with one shot.

"You have no probable cause to be here," she said. "I don't pay my taxes to have marines shutting down my security systems without warning." The marine had his rifle at hand but showed no immediate regard for Chiaki's SMG. *The arrogance*, she thought.

"I assure you, Miss Nakayama, I would not be doing this if it wasn't necessary," said Commander Pearson, tossing the megaphone into the open shuttle. "Please join me in my shuttle and I will explain the situation."

Reluctant to follow the man's orders so blindly, she decided to stall. "Why have you invaded? And are my people safe?"

"No harm will come to them as long as you play ball," said the Commander.

Chiaki wondered what she had done to put herself on the Alliance's radar. She'd struggled to pay her planet license fee a few times, but she was always able to pay it off after scrounging the web for some work. To ensure the safety of her people, she decided it best to hear out the Commander. She needed time to feel out the situation before she made any rash decisions. "Just so you know; I am not dropping my weapons." She approached him with the SMG held by her side, and the Commander said nothing.

Chiaki sat inside the Alliance shuttle, making mental notes on its internal wiring. She glanced at the command terminal, which included a self-piloting navigation system. The vehicle was capable of covering up to ten-thousand miles unassisted before needing a charge. The terminal would only follow voice commands of an Alliance marine; but Chiaki was sure she could override its permissions. She had done it once before, after all. But that was before the Alliance had updated the firmware to prevent it happening again. This shuttle wasn't capable of knocking down her security systems though, nor was it capable of outer space travel. She knew the Commander had a well-equipped ship on standby somewhere above.

"Already, I can tell we have the right person," said the Commander, seating himself. "Never has anyone looked at this heap of junk so lustfully."

"Cool it, Goldilocks!" she said. Pearson's eyebrows jumped, and then his face fell into a grimace. Chiaki's lip curled as she remembered how much she despised marines. "Just tell me why you're here, before I lose my patience."

"We have an assignment for you, Nova," he said. The use of her hacker name indicated that the Alliance was well researched. Despite her making an effort to wipe all data on herself from their systems. "Take us to the ship," the Commander said, speaking to the navigation system.

"Taking off now," it said in response.

"You want me to do a job?" she asked in response to the Commander. "Have you ever considered going through the right protocols?" The shuttle vibrated as it picked up altitude.

"If we came here on your terms to request a job then you would have the leverage to refuse. There's absolutely no room for refusals."

"So, the Alliance can now resort to taking hostages to bribe someone?" she asked. "Good to know."

The smug smile remained on the Commander's face. "This matter is of such high importance that I've been given the privilege of breaking the rules; but only where necessary, of course."

"And what if I refuse your job?" she asked. "What are you gonna do with my people?"

"I hear the C.O's at Trador are always looking for more company," said Pearson. Trador was a space station that housed the fiercest prison in the Milky Way. "Need I remind you that your entire operation is illegal?"

Chiaki scowled. "Just like this mission of yours."

"Legal or not, I'm on the side of the people that enforce the law. You have no leverage at all. Maybe you should think about getting a new line of work. I hear Ramen spots have become popular on Utrion."

Chiaki clutched the SMG and pointed it at the

Commander's groin. "You mean to tell me that Earth is all the way across the galaxy and I still have to put up with this racist shit?"

Pearson repositioned himself. "Let's start this conversation over; now that we have the initial distaste out of the way." He crossed his legs.

"Believe me," she said, "the distaste is still in the air."

He watched her for a moment before responding. "You know what? We're near the ship now; I'll brief you on the job when we get there."

They sat in silence for the ten minutes it took to reach the ship. Soon enough, she saw the giant vessel suspended in the air as the shuttle turned itself sideways to dock. A slit like opening appeared at the base of the ship to admit them.

Chiaki didn't like Alliance ships. They were too slow for her liking. But the Galactic Alliance had the money and resources to pack them full of state of the art technology; the same kind of technology that had voided her security systems. She wondered if she'd be able to get away with stealing something for later use.

"Commander Pearson has returned to the Lapwing," said the ship A.I.

Chiaki laughed. "They couldn't name your ship after a more ferocious animal?" Alliance ships were always named after animals in the Milky Way.

"A name is just a name, Nova. It's what you do with it that matters," came his response. "Please call Vraxen to the conference room," he said, as he tapped his Comm-link. Chiaki followed him, still clutching her SMG. She could feel the small star pendent—attached to the gun's handle—dance around her thigh as she walked. They reached the conference room, which was a small oval space with a control terminal in the middle and a three-sixty degree display that circled around them, cutting off at the door frame. Chiaki ran her hand through her hair as she saw herself reflected on the blank screen. She changed hairstyles often. One of her favorite styles had been when she'd had a thick, long black plat that started midway on her scalp and ran down her back. Each side of her head had been shaved low and highlighted in purple. There were so many creative ways for her to match her clothing back then. But that was a year ago; way back before her brother had died. These last few months, she'd been carrying so much grief that she'd let her hair grow natural. Today she had a small plat on the front-side of her hair, with the rest of her hair held back into a hairband.

Through the screen's reflections, she noticed Commander Pearson watching her. "Let's cut to the chase. What do you want from me?" she asked.

Pearson was about to speak when the vertical door rose. Behind him, Chiaki saw a Stowyth male enter the room. "Nova, meet your partner, Vraxen Komraz." Pearson said.

Chapter Three

"I HATE TO BREAK IT TO YOU commander, but if it's not with one of my own people, then I work alone," said Chiaki. Pearson eyed her with a condescending look that made her nostrils flare.

"I'm sorry, but it's non-negotiable. Vraxen is going with you."

In theory, it was smart of him to have someone accompany her. Not because she needed it, but because she was planning on holding the data they wanted for ransom as soon as she stole it. She would have demanded that they release her people, get off of Flade, and then pay her a hefty sum before she handed it over. Pearson knew what he was doing.

Chiaki eyed Vraxen. He was of the Stowyth species; the species that had made first-contact with humans, over a hundred years ago. Ever since that day, technology in the Milky Way had skipped generations ahead. A fusion of two different energy sources—nuclear and radox energy—had created technological advances. There were entire planets in the Milky Way being farmed for their energy and resources now. And people of Earth had migrated all across the galaxy, colonizing new planets. And the Galactic Alliance had formed to be the official governing body of the Milky Way. The Galactic Alliance was made up of four divisions: the marines, the politicians, the scientists and the trade union. Five species had a stake in founding the Galactic Alliance; humans and Stowyths were among these five species. All other species had to fend for themselves.

Vraxen stood tall, with his thick graphite skin. The Stowyths had elasticated skin that allowed them to stretch their limbs in unnatural ways. They could also withstand extreme hot and cold temperatures for far longer than humans could. Chiaki watched Vraxen's blue sclera eyes blink at her. His head was rounded with a bumpy rock-like texture. The gear that Vraxen wore, told Chiaki that he wasn't part of the Alliance. He had to be a mercenary.

"You better tell him to stay out of my way," she said.

The Stowyth said something in his native tongue of Quabic. "Translating Quabic," said Tobi, who had found a way to connect to the ship's network.

After a few seconds, the Comm-link had downloaded the Quabic dictionary to its memory. It repeated Vraxen's words back to Chiaki in English, using a sample of the Stowyths own voice. "You focus on your task and I'll focus on mine." Vraxen had said, with a raspy voice.

"And just what is your task?" she asked. Silence followed. A silence that confirmed he was only there to watch her and make sure she didn't disobey the Alliance.

"Let's first talk about yours," said Commander Pearson. "We need you to bust into a data center on a planet known as New Yoy and extract some Intel for us."

"New what?"

"New Yoy," Pearson repeated, as if ready for the question. "A planet that only the Alliance and its inhabitants are aware of."

The name made Chiaki wonder just how much classified information the Alliance held. If there was a New Yoy then that meant there was an Old Yoy. She would have probed on, but she had a more pressing question. "What kind of Intel are we talking?"

"New Yoy is home to a band of terrorists that we've been monitoring. We call them the Thundercloaks."

Chiaki raised an eyebrow. "Wow, how did Alliance lames like you come up with such a name?"

Pearson smirked. "The planet is in a constant state of thunder, and the terrorists wear cloaks."

She rolled her eyes, "that's some genius shit."

"To make a long story short; we need to know what the Thundercloaks are planning. We're aware of a dangerous plot unraveling; one that could threaten the entire structure of the Milky Way."

Chiaki's faith in the Galactic Alliance was so minute that she had to decide how much of this information to filter out of her brain. "Why do you need me? I'm not the only hacker in the galaxy. I hear the Alliance is hiring some of the most infamous hackers these days." Many of the hacker groups that Chiaki and her brother had competed on jobs with were now hired by the Alliance, incarcerated or dead.

"The complexity of the programming is advanced. We know that you're responsible for cracking the Mars Excelsior security system." The Excelsior was a galaxy-wide banking and stock market firm. Chiaki was once hired to break into their system. She'd only agreed to penetrate its security for the challenge and had refused to steal anything. The Excelsior was used by millions of innocent people, and she wanted no part in taking money from them. Instead, she'd set up a login for the client to do whatever they wished. After they'd paid her the second half of her score, they were free to do as they pleased with the account; or so they thought. Chiaki had later regretted granting the client access, and she'd seen to it that the client was caught for a separate crime. Having the client locked up had done wonders for Chiaki's confidence. With every job she accepted, there was moral anxiety that she would have to overcome. The Excelsior job had been too big of a moral challenge for her.

Chiaki wanted to be careful how she responded to Pearson here. She didn't want to clearly own up to such a crime. "If what you say is true, then why am I not locked up?" she asked.

"We knew the time would come when we'd need

you."

This was exactly why she despised the Alliance. They knew about the dirt that happened in the galaxy but instead of acting on what they knew, they would leverage it for their own gain. Chiaki would prefer they break down her door and arrest her than using her in this way.

"Whatever," she said, losing the will to argue. "I charge five-hundred-thousand credits for such a job."

Vraxen grunted from beside Pearson. "There will be no commission," said the Commander.

"Then there's no deal," she said, clutching her SMG. "Bring me back home and release my people."

"I'm under strict orders to not commission you," he said. "But how does this sound?"

"Go on."

"We have information on your brother's murder, and I will share what we know after the job is complete."

Chiaki processed this for some time. It only contributed further to her dislike of the Alliance. But if there was one thing she couldn't dismiss, it was the chance to bring peace to the memory of her brother.

"Understand that I hate you for this; but we have a deal, Commander."

Pearson extended his hand and Chiaki shook it.

CHAPTER FOUR

WITH THE LAPWING ripping its way through space, Chiaki now had access to the network via the ship's router. She'd already attempted to hack into the Alliance network to obtain some data. She'd hoped to find the information on her brother that Pearson had spoken of. Unfortunately, they had been wise enough to cut the ship off from the Alliance mainframe. The only data she could find was the Lapwing's local files, which mainly consisted of diagnostics and logs of no interest.

She resorted to looking up anything she could find about the Thundercloaks online. She made sure to plug her VPN module into her Comm-link so that nobody could find out what she was browsing.

"Sorry, Nova, all I can find on the Thundercloaks is a series of space operas. If you like, I can read them to you," said Tobi.

"That's fine, try to find all known locations of Galactic Alliance data centers," she said. The A.I returned a list of locations to her Comm-link display. Reluctant to record any of this information, she committed it to her memory for later use.

Chiaki then slept for hours in her quarters; ignoring all invitations to eat in the kitchen. Though she was hungry, Chiaki refused to eat anything provided by the Alliance.

The Alliance ship had level five FTL travel, the fastest level of FTL available in the Milky Way. This meant that the Lapwing could get from one side of the galaxy to the other in a matter of days. On Chiaki's own ship, it would take her a couple of weeks to go from one corner of the Milky Way to the other because she only had level two FTL installed. Even with the Lapwings speed, Chiaki still had enough time to enjoy her nap.

When she woke, she played one of her favorite music artists, Minmi, and practiced her Wing Chun. Eventually, Pearson's voice made the announcement that they would reach New Yoy in two hours. He advised Chiaki and Vraxen to ready themselves and invited them to request equipment from the armory.

Chiaki's lack of trust for the Alliance extended to the use of their weapons. She remembered reading somewhere that the Alliance was beginning to implement chips into their weapons that would prevent guns from firing on anyone associated with the Alliance. Even if it was meant as a safety measure, she knew that such a thing could be manipulated.

With her SMG and her hidden blade, there was a chance she may be under-equipped for the job, but she would make do. She squeezed herself back into her skinsuit. The suit was all black on the outside, with synthetic padding all over to protect herself from knocks and bumps. The suit had a magnetized waistline that would keep her SMG within reach without holsters or any kind of binding. She had customized the skinsuit by sealing in strips of neon lights that she could switch on and off at will. She could re-program the color of these lights with her Comm-link anytime she wanted. Not only did the lights help to display her personality, but they also gave her some relief when it came to her fear of the dark.

Chiaki popped the Comm-link back on her wrist and pulled on her gloves. She then equipped a visor on her head and placed a breather around her neck so it was ready when she needed it. The breather was a standard piece of equipment that every traveler in the Milky Way needed; in case they found themselves in areas where no oxygen mills were set up. The breather was a synthetic elasticated material that fit around the nose and mouth. Chiaki's breather was customized so that it displayed the image of a skull's nose and mouth over where her own would be.

The voice of Commander Pearson beamed through the speakers once more, causing Chiaki to jump. "Would Miss Nakayama and Mr. Komraz please report to the conference room for a final briefing."

Chiaki entered the conference room once again to find Commander Pearson and Vraxen. "You must arm yourself, Nova," said Pearson.

"I am armed!" she snapped back. "What do we need to discuss?"

"There are a number of powerful modded

weapons in the armory for you to use," he said.

"I will do my best to protect you," Vraxen added. "But you must prepare for the worst." Now that Chiaki's Comm-link had Vraxen's language and voice sample, his speech could be translated in real-time.

"I appreciate the concern, but I'm capable of looking after myself. And I don't need the Alliance's overpowered artillery to do it. All that crap is designed for people who can't be civil," she responded. Vraxen blinked at her.

"Let me be clear, Miss Nakayama, failure is not an option here. The Thundercloaks are no joke, please take this mission seriously."

Chiaki's eyes thinned. "Did you take my people back on Flade seriously, Commander?" There was a pause. "Exactly, so don't tell me what I should take seriously. Until you've let my people go."

"It's alright, Commander," said Vraxen. "I will take extra precautions to ensure her safety on the mission." Chiaki disliked the idea of having someone breathing down her neck while she worked.

"Indeed, Vraxen, and that was one of the things on my list. You must stay close together at all times, and never separate under any circumstances," said Pearson. "If you run into any Thundercloaks, report to me immediately if the situation allows it. We would prefer if they never even knew you were there, but we don't know the extent of their precautions. Our Intel shows that this building isn't heavily guarded, as they have moved to a new data center. They did however; leave many records behind at this one. There was somewhat of a fallout between parties, so much of their data hasn't been transferred to the new location. But even with this facility being the old one, you should still expect to come across drones and android sentries."

"Those things are toys to me," said Chiaki.

"Indeed; this makes you even more suited for the job."

Chiaki chose not to let the comment boost her ego. The last thing she needed was to be complimented by the Alliance. "Once everything is good on the ground level, how do we get inside the data center?" she asked.

Pearson cleared his throat. "We suspect that the front door is digitally secured. It shouldn't be a problem for you, but be warned that the door is likely programed to send a notification when the door is opened. You'll have to prevent that notification from being sent."

"Noted," she said.

Commander Pearson walked over to a cabinet and removed a small round device. "Take this," he said, passing it to Chiaki. "It's an infra-red sensor that you can place on the wall once inside. Pair it with your Comm-link to get an idea of any threats lurking inside. It will also show you the locations of all electronic devices. Look for the server room, that's where you should find the mainframe."

"Sounds good," said Chiaki.

Pearson removed an SD card from his pocket and handed it to Chiaki. "Download the data to this, and hand it over to Vraxen on completion," he said. Chiaki's lip curled at the order to hand the card over to Vraxen. "Be advised that on ground level, the building looks around three stories high," he continued. "But to access the data archives, you'll actually need to go a few levels below the surface."

"You mean the building goes underground?

That's pretty smart," she said.

"I'll be standing by for communication over the Comm-link; should you need to ask anything." Chiaki secretly hoped there would be no reason to contact him at all. "Are there any final questions?" asked Pearson.

"What about landing and extraction?" Chiaki asked. With it being a stealth mission, shuttling in could easily catch someone's attention.

"You'll have to parachute in, unfortunately," said Pearson. "But don't worry; I'll have an Astrid shuttle to extract you both with." An Astrid was a weaponized shuttle used for entering hostile territories.

"What about oxygen mills?" she asked. Oxygen mills allowed organics to breath air on planets that didn't have a natural output of the element. If a planet didn't have oxygen mills set up then you would need to rely on breathers to keep you alive.

"There are oxygen mills in place, so no need to worry about breathers," said Pearson. He looked down at his Comm-link. "We'll be there in forty minutes now. I need a private word with Vraxen here. Feel free to make any last minute preparations, Miss Nakayama."

"Thank god, I've had enough of you, Goldilocks," she said, dashing for the exit.

With every new job, came a level of excitement. Chiaki loved a challenge, but something about this job was making her feel uneasy. She wasn't sure if it was the thought of having someone breathing over her shoulder, or the fact that her employer was the Galactic Alliance. Maybe it was both those things; but one thing was for certain, and that was that Chiaki had to know why this mission was so important to the G.A.

CHAPTER FIVE

COMMANDER PEARSON LED CHIAKI and Vraxen to the shuttle bay on the Lapwing's lower level. It was here where Chiaki caught a glimpse of the Astrid that would be extracting them. It was a long vessel with rotor wings and four sloped legs. Machine guns were attached to the vehicles front legs.

Commander Pearson pressed his palm against the security panel on one of the other shuttles to activate it. "Open up," he said. Immediately, the shuttle doors rose to admit them. Chiaki and Vraxen stepped inside and began strapping themselves in.

"The shuttle will carry you to twelve-thousand feet above ground level. From there you'll need to free fall and activate your chutes, which can be found beside your seats," said Pearson. "Don't forget to put them on before you jump."

"You think I'm an amateur earthling or something?" Chiaki asked.

Pearson smirked. "Well, this is it, good luck. Please send word once you've landed." Pearson's face disappeared as the shuttle doors closed.

There was momentary darkness, until the shuttle lights blinked on. Vraxen's midnight blue eyes were locked onto Chiaki, making her uncomfortable. It didn't help that the Stowyth's entire sclera was blue, giving him a menacing look.

"Something you wanna say, Vraxy?" she asked.

"It's Vraxen," he breathed.

"Duh!" she rolled her eyes. "Which planet are you from anyway?" She asked, because the Stowyths weren't restricted to any one planet in the Milky Way. They had colonized a number of planets, long before humans had made first-contact with them.

"That is not relevant to the mission," he said.

Chiaki sighed. It was going to be a long day. Being sent on this mission against her will and being stuck with a Stowyth that lacked any social skills was enough to send her over the edge. The only thing keeping her sane was the curiosity of finding out what kind of data the G.A were after, and why they needed it so badly that they'd hire her. More than that, she wanted to know what Pearson had on her brothers' murder. She needed a new lead, and now Pearson was handing it to her on a platter.

"Utrion," said Vraxen, now blinking frantically. "I used to live on Utrion."

Utrion was a planet colonized by humans, Stowyths and Garrues. It was looked at as a planet where the lowest of the low in each of the races went to make a life. It was a poverty driven cesspool, with a thriving underworld. Things were so bad there that the Galactic Alliance found it a waste of time to police the planet. Instead, the planet had its own corrupted lawmakers.

"It's not often that someone from Utrion ends up working with the Alliance," said Chiaki.

Vraxen's eyelids locked together for some time. "Pearson saved my life," he said, slowly opening his eyes. "I owe him."

"You mean that lameass was able to save your life?" she asked, raising an eyebrow. "You seem way more competent than he is."

"He didn't do it physically," he said, rubbing his neck. "He struck a deal with a loan shark that was out to kill me. Pearson paid off my debt for me."

Chiaki knew that loan sharks ran rampant on Utrion. "Why'd you even go to a loan shark on that planet?"

"I do not wish to speak about this," said Vraxen, inhaling air sharply.

Now approaching twelve-thousand feet, said the shuttle.

Chiaki unbuckled her restraint as she felt the shuttle slowing down. She grabbed the parachute beside her seat and placed it behind her.

"Here, let me help you," said Vraxen, reaching for her parachute straps.

"No, I got it," she snapped, reluctant to let him touch her. Vraxen's eyelids reduced to slits at the rejection.

The Stowyth stood and threw his own parachute over his back, quickly fastening the straps over his chest. "We must jump together, holding each other by the arm. We cannot risk being separated."

"How about we just stay close; there's no need to hold hands, honey," said Chiaki.

"Just don't get lost. I don't want to babysit you through the mission." Chiaki's nose wrinkled at his words. "Pop down your visor. You humans have fragile eyes; I don't want you to injure them during the fall."

Chiaki slid the eye guard on her visor down.

We have reached parachute level; now opening the doors. Please watch your step.

Chiaki and Vraxen walked to the door and stood side by side. When the door opened, they were hit with a blast of wind that had them stumbling back. "Whoa, Pearson wasn't kidding about the thunder here," said Chiaki, as she watched bolts of lightning rip through the skies.

"We'll have to be careful. Stay close." Vraxen looked over at Chiaki. "On the count of three," he said, holding three fingers in the air.

"Three," he dropped one finger.

"Two," another finger fell.

Before he could drop the third, Chiaki nudged him aside and threw herself out the shuttle doors. The wind whipped against her face as she descended through the skies of this planet that she didn't know existed. She was happy to finally steal a moment alone; it had been her plan, to try and separate from Vraxen as soon as she got a chance. She didn't need him ruining her fun.

Chiaki admired the wet autumn leaves on the fast approaching trees.

"Lean to your side a little to stay on path," Tobi said, through her earpiece. She followed his instruction until she found herself nearing parachute activation level. She moved her hand over the switch, readying herself for the landing. For a moment, she felt lost in time. She thought about her brother Kura and wondered if he was able to fly like this in the afterlife. And then a thought occurred to her—if she didn't use her parachute, she could see her brother again. All she had to do was endure the momentary pain of her body colliding with the ground. Perhaps she could aim for a tree to break the fall slightly. But then there was the possibility her breaking her neck instead and suffering immensely as a result. She wasn't sure she had the guts to go through with it.

She would never know if she would have gone

through with the idea, because just then, she felt something grab her by the arm. Vraxen had found his way to her and he slapped her activation switch aggressively with his other hand, causing the parachute to rip out of its pack behind her. Chiaki was then lifted vertically and she felt the pace of her descent slow. Vraxen activated his own parachute and was gliding beside her, his eyes locked on her and his nostrils flared. "What were you thinking?" he yelled.

"Maybe I wanted to see how good you were at your job." Chiaki smiled.

"This is not a game," he said, "come, swing right, our location is to the east."

Within a minute, they'd both landed, just a few feet away from one another. They were in a forest, full of fallen autumn leaves. The ground was plastered with mud. "It's so beautiful here," Chiaki said, "reminds me of Earth."

"I've never been," said Vraxen.

"You kidding me?"

"Humans are too inquisitive; I'd rather not be on your home planet."

"Hey, don't make generalizations, kiddo."

Vraxen sneered at her, before raising his left arm and tapping his Comm-link. "Commander, we've landed," he said, "sending you our co-ordinates now." He then reached into one of the many pockets on his space armor and pulled out a Stowyth earpiece. He placed it on a curve behind his head, which was where Stowyth's received sound.

Within seconds, both their devices received calls from Commander Pearson. They both answered and the Comm-link system automatically sorted them into a group call.

"Well done on the landing," said Pearson. *"Quickly dispose of your parachutes and try not to draw any attention to yourselves. You'll need to walk an estimate of twenty minutes uphill to reach the data center from your position. You landed farther out than intended."*

"That may not be a bad thing. It means we can scout the building and make sure there aren't any nasty surprises," said Varxen.

"Precisely; watch your back, and send word once you reach the center."

Chiaki and Vraxen proceeded to tuck their parachutes back into their packs. They stashed their packs under some leaves by the side of the path. Chiaki slid her visor up and took a deep breath. The air felt thick and fresh; and suddenly Chiaki was full of purpose. It was as if the intake of fresh oxygen had hit her brain and given her a dose of motivation. "Let's get going, boulder-face."

His eyes narrowed. "Come, short girl."

Chiaki strutted alongside the Stowyth, smiling. "That was the lamest comeback I ever heard."

CHAPTER SIX

CHIAKI SLOWED INTO A CROUCH, creeping up towards the large carbon steel structure.

"I hear something," said Vraxen. Stowyth's were known to have sharper senses than humans.

"What kind of sound is it?"

Vraxen tilted his head. "It sounds mechanical," he said. "I believe it's a drone."

"A security drone, huh?" Chiaki could easily hack a security drone, but she needed to get it in her hands first. Getting it was the hard part, because most security drones would send out an alert on any sign of impact. "I need to get my hands on it. I can reprogram it so that it covers our backs. Then, instead of it alerting these thunder-assholes, it will alert us if someone shows up."

"If I shoot it down it will alert them," said Vraxen. "You should have taken some EMPs from the Lapwing; I told you it was a bad idea to not come prepared."

Chiaki rolled her eyes. "Cry me a river, Vraxy. The Alliance aren't the only ones with tools." She reached into a small compartment, located on the left thigh of her suit. "Nova always comes prepared," she said, pulling a small marble shaped ball from the compartment. It was a metallic object, with a mini magnet strip on one of its curved edges. "All I need is for you to catch the drone," she pointed. "After I toss this on it, it's gonna hit the dirt fast. Think you can do your stretchy limb thing to get it before it shatters to a million pieces?"

"What is that thing?" he asked.

"It's a mini-EMP. Good enough to shut down small, mobile electronics. But it's too small to shut down anything over two-hundred volts."

Chiaki waited, until she saw the drone fly into sight while circling the building. She counted to three before throwing the object at the drone. The EMP attached itself to the drone and they heard a mechanical click as the device was shut down.

Vraxen demonstrated the abilities of a healthy Stowyth by running forward and stretching his arms out to catch the drone as it spiraled from the sky.

Chiaki knew she had just a minute to work her magic, before the effects of the EMP wore off.

"Set it down," she said, jogging to Vraxen. With the drone on the ground, she opened a compartment on the side of her Comm-link that housed a GSB connector. She popped the cable into the drone's frame, under its four propellers. It was now connected to her Comm-link. "Tobi, run my drone re-write code."

"Shall I include your latest patch, even though you've yet to finish it?" Tobi asked.

"No, just run the vanilla version," she said.

"Why vanilla?" Vraxen asked, "you don't like flavor?"

Chiaki swallowed hard. "Just let me work." With her own software now running on her display, she used the on-screen controls on her Comm-link to scroll through the drone's functions. Her customized software allowed her to add in her own modifications at the tap of a finger. It also translated any code that was written with a different language. In the Milky Way, one programming language was widely used, but that coding language had at least ten language variations. A hacker would have a tough time if they didn't have an auto-translate software at the ready. Chiaki's only worry now was that the EMP would wear off before she found the alert function. "Dammit, where is it."

"Chiaki, you have twenty-five seconds until the EMP wears off," said Tobi.

"Screw it," said Chiaki. She hit a macro key that she'd programmed to run a find and replace command. Typically, she avoided using the command as it took too long to load and then she would need to either type in or speak what she's looking for. In this case, it was taking too long for her to scroll through the drone's programming, so maybe the risk would be worth it. "Find the word '*alert*'," she told Tobi.

"There are zero instances of the word *alert*," he said.

"Shit, they're smart with their coding." The lack of the word in the code meant that the Thundercloaks had taken precautions, masking the names of its functions to give hackers a hard time. To narrow down her search to the alert function, she simply needed to think of a variable that only pertained to the alert feature. "Tobi, find *sendto*," she asked. This would look up any instances where data is being sent to a third-party from the drone.

"Six instances of the term *sendto* have been returned." Chiaki quickly scrolled through the six instances, searching for anything that looked like a security alert. She saw that there were functions to send diagnostics and weather conditions at two hour intervals.

Finally, something caught her attention. There was a function called ***notifyElf***. Inside the function was a condition called ***OnStrike***. Usually, a drone's alert condition would be named ***OnContact*** but she guessed that the programmers had renamed the condition for inconvenience. "This has to be it," she said.

"Five seconds until the EMP is disabled," said Tobi. Chiaki quickly input comment tags around the function to prevent it from working. "EMP disabled," said Tobi.

Chiaki saw Vraxen's head tilt through the corner of her eye. "Did it work?" he asked. At that moment, the drone came back to life below them, its propellers turning slowly. Chiaki quickly hit the switch to disable flight mode.

"If the alert was working, this red light would blink to indicate that it's sending data." She pointed to the red light on the drone's tail.

"Excellent," he said. "Let's continue on."

"Give me one moment," said Chiaki. "I still have to reset the alert so that it will come to us instead." With no danger of an alert being sent, Chiaki could now take her time to modify the code. She re-wrote all *sendto* actions so that they would instead send data to her Comm-link.

"You think these guys might be *Lord of the Rings* fans or something?" she asked, wondering why the alert function had been named *notifyElf*. Could it be that these *Thundercloaks* were as nerdy as she was?

"You are asking me things that I know nothing about," he said.

She shook her head. "None of you non-human species give Earth entertainment its due diligence."

Once Chiaki had finished re-writing the drone's code, she reactivated its flight mode and watched it soar into the skies. "Now we'll know whenever something moves within its range."

"Good," said Vraxen. "Now you must work your magic on this door."

Thankfully, disabling the alert on the door was easy now that she knew the *notifyElf* function. She had used another EMP widget, but she was running low on her supply. With the front door alert disabled all she needed was to get it to open.

"How long will this take?" Vraxen asked as another bolt of lightning rippled through the skies. A barrage of thunder sounds followed.

"You're not scared of a little thunder, are you Vraxy?" she said, kneeling by the door while operating her Comm-link.

"Please, do not call me that."

Chiaki disregarded Vraxen and brought her attention back to the task at hand. Since the door responded to a biometric authentication system, she would need to re-write the authentication code so that it would trick the door into opening up for them. There was only one problem...

"Shit, these scripts are all encrypted."

"What does that mean?" Vraxen asked.

"Tobi, run my script cracker," she said. When she saw the program open up on her Comm-link, she glanced back at Vraxen. "It means that this could take a while."

Vraxen's dark lips curled, revealing his platinum shaded teeth. "Now I know why I'm not a hacker," he grunted.

"Wanna know the secret of the Milky Way?" she asked him. She continued without waiting for a response, "Patience. If you learn patience, you'll learn everything there is to know about this galaxy before your demise."

Vraxen blinked. "If that's the case, why don't you know who killed your brother?"

Chiaki twitched. She breathed in and out to calm herself. "Some people are good at covering their tracks. I'll find them eventually."

"With the help of the Alliance, the organization you harbor so much hatred for?"

"Chī shǐ, shithead," she snapped, cursing him with her slang. On her wrist, she saw that the script cracker was still trying to break the encryption.

Arrays of symbols that represented the encrypted characters were slowly formulating into their correct arrangements.

"My mother fell sick," said Vraxen. "That's why I went to the loan sharks on Utrion. I needed enough money to buy her medicine and pay for her treatments." Vraxen cupped his hands together, rubbing his palms. "They gave me enough money to keep her treatments going for five years. They said I wouldn't have to start paying them back for two years. I didn't even know how I was going to pay them back; I just wanted to keep my mother alive. I told myself I would figure it out later. But then—." Vraxen paused, his head panning towards the sky. "My mother died a year into her treatment."

Chiaki closed her eyes briefly. "I'm sorry." She too had lost her parents many years ago. She and Kura had traveled to space from Earth as orphans.

"Since I'd only used a years' worth of the money, I offered to give the loan sharks back the rest of what they gave to me. But they were unreasonable. They said they wanted it all paid back with interest, in one lump sum. They gave me just a month to come up with one-hundred Utrion Orbs and two-hundred-thousand credits."

Utrion Orbs were a currency exclusive to the Utrion ecosystem, whereas credits were a universal currency used across the Milky Way. It was foul of the loan sharks to ask for absurd amounts of money across two different currencies, in just one month.

"Of course, I was in no position to pay. My only options were to steal a number of weapons from an outpost and use them to protect myself every time the mercs caught up to me. This one time I was at a bar, wallowing in my sorrows. Some mercs came to collect or assassinate me. I managed to fight them off in a skirmish that completely destroyed the bar. Commander Pearson had been watching me the whole time. That was when he asked to recruit me for his cause, in exchange for paying off my debts."

Chiaki could just imagine Pearson watching the fight with that smug look on his face; not even thinking about intervening. With his authority, he could have ended the fight anytime he wanted. The thought sickened her.

"I know you have your reservations about the

Alliance, but they do help people. In many ways," he said.

"So basically, your leash was handed over from one master to another," she said. "You're wasting your best years, Vraxy. You could be free, like me."

Vraxen exhaled deeply through the slits on his face.

"Nova, the code is fully decrypted," said Tobi.

"Finally," she said. She scanned through the code and made the necessary modifications. All that was left was for her to take a picture so that the system would recognize her face and proceed to give her entry. When the Comm-link camera blinked, she closed an eye-lid and stuck her tongue out. A clicking noise indicated that the photo had been taken.

"Seriously, how old are you?" Vraxen asked.

Chiaki ignored him and wrote some additional code that would wipe her picture from the system after two hours. When she was done, she ran the authenticator and the door came back to life.

"Okay, we're in business. Let's go, Vraxy."

"Please, stop that," he said, walking towards the door.

Chiaki stood and faced the biometric camera on the side of the door. She replicated the expression from her photo and the door slid upwards to admit them.

CHAPTER SEVEN

CHIAKI PACED HER STEPS as she entered the dark and dank hallway. Her nose wrinkled at the vile smell. "It smells like carcasses in here," she said.

She heard Vraxen take large intake of breath through the nose. "It's just animals," he said.

They moved towards a railing and Chiaki peered over the side. Below was an indoor garden full of dead plants and flowers; an attempt to make the building more environmental when it was inhabited. She could see that there were two squared railings below their level, indicating that there were two more floors below them. And probably even more floors that they couldn't see.

"Use the infra-red," said Vraxen.

She removed the round device from her pocket and pushed in the button on it's underside for three seconds; it bleeped to indicate that it was on. She tapped the same button again to pair the device to her Comm-link. On her Comm-link, she used the scanner to receive the device's signal. The device bleeped once more to confirm that it was paired. Chiaki then slammed the device against the panel below the railing. On her Comm-link she could now see a feed that showed all energy sources in the building as red dots. There were an abundance of computers on the levels below them; as well as fans, heaters, drones and other appliances.

"Look," said Vraxen, pointing to something on her Comm-link screen. "There are floors even lower than the garden."

"No shit," she said, "and look there." She pointed to a moving energy source that was way below them. "With how big that dot is and with how it's moving, it could only be a security droid."

"We will need to proceed carefully."

Chiaki used the scroll wheel on her Comm-link to pan the feed. "Right there," she pointed. "The security droid is right by a ton of red dots. That has to be the server room, and that's where the mainframe will be."

"Okay, keep that feed running. We'll use it to guide us. At least we'll know when something is coming."

Chiaki disregarded Vraxen's words and looked around her, from left to right. She made a mental note of the ventilation duct to the far right of the platform.

"What are you looking at?" he asked.

Chiaki said nothing. She wondered how quick Vraxen's reflexes were. "Aren't you tired of being a babysitter?" she asked, taking three steps back. "Surely, running from loan sharks would have been more fun than this." His head tilted and the slits of his eyes tightened.

Chiaki reached into one of her suit pockets. By the time Vraxen registered her movement she had slammed a smoke pellet on the platform. Waves of smoke shot into the air and Chiaki heard violent wails that she guessed were Stowyth coughs.

She ran across the opposite side of the platform, putting as much distance between herself and Vraxen as she could before he could catch up to her. When she reached the caged ventilation entrance, she stole a glance behind her. Vraxen was emerging from the smoke, his eyes wide with disbelief.

Chiaki pulled on the top-right corner of the cage

as hard as she could until she felt it shift.

"His Comm-link signal is getting stronger, Nova," said Tobi, trying to make her aware of the Stowyth's distance.

She pulled the bottom corner now; being too careful not to break a nail. Vraxen's feet were pounding the aluminum platform behind her. She gasped, as the cage finally ripped apart from the duct opening. Without looking behind her, she held onto the top crevice of the opening and threw her legs inside. Vraxen's arm went through the hole after her, as the duct swallowed her body.

Chiaki felt herself sliding down the curved slopes. She was able to spread her feet and slow her descent before the final bend that would take her two floors below. Her chest pounded as the adrenaline in her body slowed. But it wasn't the time to be calm, because as she glanced up the duct, she witnessed Vraxen's arm stretching itself down the duct, feeling its way around for her.

"Shit!" she whispered.

"Why do this, Nova?" came his voice, echoing down the duct.

She shuffled her body down the curve until she was resting on her back. Another cage was blocking her exit. She slammed her foot against the cage and applied pressure. When it didn't budge, she continued slamming her foot against it.

Suddenly, she felt Vraxen's arm slide against her hair. He was feeling around, deciding which part of her body would be the most appropriate to grab. At least he had some level of respect. After bypassing her hair and her neck, he soon found her underarm and decided he would try to pull her up by it. Chiaki felt her body shift and she lost some of the reach she needed to continue kicking the cage open.

"Leave me alone!" she yelled. She heard her own voice trailing up the duct and Vraxen loosened his grip in response.

She took advantage by slipping her body further down the bend, condensing her already small body. She leaned on her side and kicked the cage with her free foot; kicking harder each time.

Finally, she felt the cage shifting.

"We need to stick together, that droid is dangerous." She heard.

The cage crashed to the floor as Vraxen's hand reached her again. She wasted no time shuffling her body out of the opening.

For a moment, she considered trying to bind the cage back over the hole. She thought that maybe Vraxen could push himself down after her. But although his limbs were flexible, the rest of his body mass would be too bulky.

"Sorry, Vraxy; catch you later," she said.

When she turned, she was now facing the garden full of dead plants. The foul stench made her lip curl. A shuffling sound came from the floors above and Chiaki ran to the first door on her left in response. She felt somewhat bad for ditching Vraxen after hearing his story; but he was loyal to Pearson and that meant he was ultimately against her.

When she entered the room, a light sensor turned on. She noticed cameras, but after some inspection she realized they were off. There were rows of computers in front of her, and the sight of them raised her spirits. To Chiaki, computers meant purpose and possibilities. There were always new things to discover when entering a room full of computers away from her home on Flade.

Before turning on the computers, she tip-toed over the sides of the tables, observing where the cables led. She saw that they were all connected to a hub at the other side of the room.

"Chiaki, it would seem that these computers are on a separate network from the sever rooms below," said Tobi.

"I think you're right," she said, walking to one of the computers. Clearly these computers were all hooked up to their own private network, the questions was whether each computer would boot into its local desktop or if it would boot right into the network login screen. As expected, the screen blinked right into the network's login screen. This meant that Chiaki would need to hack the network connection from the hub first. From there, she could figure out how to obtain an admin login for herself.

"Tobi," she said, as she connected her Comm-link to the hub. "Once I crack this, I'll need you to read out any data you can find that's relevant to the Thundercloaks, New Yoy or the Galactic Alliance. I won't have time to sit around here reading everything."

"Noted," said Tobi.

The way connections worked in the Milky Way was that satellites and spaceships allowed for mobile and Comm-link devices to access their own wireless technologies. Through these built-in technologies, one would have access to the galaxy-wide Internet service. It was then up to individuals and corporations on each planet to secure their own private networks so nobody could access their data. As of now, Tobi was able to access the galaxy-wide Internet, thanks to New Yoy's satellite, but once Chiaki worked her magic, he would be able to explore whatever data was stored on the private network in the room they now stood in.

Without Vraxen there to break her concentration, Chiaki was able to focus entirely on her cracker software. When she'd hacked the door earlier, she'd had to rely completely on the software's automated feature. But with no distraction, she could manually input characters alongside the automated cracker to try and figure out the login faster.

It took her around five minutes to crack the login, and she used it to set up her own user login with full access to the network. She did the initial setup from her Comm-link, but decided to test out her new user login on one of the computers. Only then did she see that she didn't recognize the language written on screen, all she knew was that there were two text boxes, one for Username and one for Password.

"Nova, I'm picking up Vraxen's signal again," said Tobi.

"Dammit," she said, as she watched the computer log onto the network successfully. "Alright, Tobi, scan the network and read me anything you find." She turned the computer off and crept over to the window facing the garden. There was no sign of movement so she crept through the door and dashed for the room on the other side of the floor, in search for a way down below.

CHAPTER EIGHT

THE ROOM WAS DARK, leaving Chiaki on edge. There was something about the dark that made her uneasy. In the dark, she had no control over the uncanny. She was so used to being able to manipulate things around her that she just couldn't deal with the hopeless feeling of being in darkness.

The room would have to stay dark for now because a drone had hovered in from the other side, as if emerging from nowhere. Chiaki guessed the stairway to the levels below was somewhere back there. She pressed her back against a set of cabinets, wondering why the room didn't have a light sensor like the last one. It wasn't a good idea to activate the neon light strips on her skinsuit in case the drone detected her. She was forced to somehow get past the drone in darkness and silence. She was unable to talk to Tobi, as she was close enough to the drone to have her voice picked up, but thankfully, Tobi would be able to speak to her through the headset. There wasn't much he could do in terms of detecting the drone's signal, because it worked differently from a Comm-link signal. But she hoped he would speak to her eventually so that she didn't feel so alone in this situation. She had just ditched Vraxen to be alone, and now she wished she wasn't; the irony.

She peered around the side of the cabinet, watching and listening. Her ears told her that the drone was behind her to the left. There seemed to be some hall lighting in the distance on her right. That was where she needed to be. She could probably make it downstairs without dealing with the drone at all, but if Vraxen was clumsy enough to be discovered by it, it could put her life in jeopardy. The question was, did she want to destroy the drone or hack it? She had just one mini-EMP left at her disposal. She wouldn't be able to use the EMP on the android downstairs because androids were too high voltage; but who knew what else she may need it for later?

She made the decision to destroy this one. This meant that she'd need to get behind it and catch it by surprise. Drones had a high sensitivity for noise and could send alerts within five seconds of detecting something. But Chiaki knew that security drones had what was called a suspicious filter built in. This was an algorithm that assessed whether a noise may have been made by a conscious species or an animal. Too often, wild animals would trigger a drone's alert system and spam its owner with false warnings. That was why the suspicious filter algorithm was created, so the drone would have some sense of judgment.

After hours of trolling her own drones, Chiaki figured out that she could distract a drone by making distant sounds as long as there wasn't too much impact behind it. Chiaki took the micro-SMG from her hip, trying extra hard not to make any noise. She fiddled with the bottom of the handle, where her star pendant was attached. The drone's hovering was getting nearer. Finally, she had the pendant detached and as she looked down at it in her palm, she hoped not to lose it. Her brother had given it to her long ago.

Chiaki tossed the pendant across the room and heard it make contact with a cabinet. The drone's hover paused, and she heard the mechanical sound of it doing a three-sixty turn. She could see the reflection from its search light as it hovered to the source of the sound. If the drone had thought the noise came from a conscious species, the alert would have already been sent and she'd be in big trouble.

With the drone now facing the other way and its search light providing enough light to aim, she stood and raised her SMG, aiming for the weak point where its frame connected. The drone must have heard her movement, as its red light blinked, initiating the five second alert phase. She squeezed the trigger in panic, feeling the bullets tear out the nozzle. The drone collapsed and shattered on the ground. She tip-toed over the cabinet to see what state the drone was in before approaching, she didn't want to be picked up by it's camera if it was still functioning. Thankfully, the drone appeared to be completely offline.

She ran around the set of cabinets to retrieve her pendant and then she ran towards the right side of the room. She didn't want to linger around here too long after opening fire, even though her SMG was good at suppressing noise.

She found herself in a tight corridor with a blinking light. There was an elevator on the right side, but she didn't want to take the risk of using it.

"Nova!" Tobi called in her ear.

"Oh there you are. Where were you when I needed comfort?"

"Sorry, but you told me to find useful data. If you need me to multitask then I need more RAM, you know how this works."

"Oh, I see your sassy module is working fine," she said. "What do you have for me?"

She had now reached the stairway. It was the kind of stairway that spiraled. She decided not to go down while she was talking to Tobi, in case her voice was picked up. She moved closer to the elevator and leaned against the wall opposite it.

"There are many logs that are written in languages not recognized, but I've managed to find some in languages that can be translated. I will read one now," said Tobi.

"Go for it."

Thanks to the traveler's appearance, we now know that the loss of our ancient power was at the command of our ancestors from Yoyvis. Though we'd heard of the planet's demise long ago, we never knew that others from the planet had escaped before it was destroyed. It seems they blamed magic for the death of Yoyvis and thus they wished to cast it away. Simply put, I believe that landing on Earth poisoned their minds.

"What does this all mean?" she asked, once Tobi stopped talking. "He mentions somewhere called Yoyvis, so I'm guessing that's the old-Yoy, right?"

"That is my guess," said Tobi.

"And he talks about an ancient power, and magic? Are you sure he wasn't writing Potter fan-fic or something?"

"Potter is only considered a classic peace of twenty-first century literature on Earth..."

"Yeah, I know that," she said. "But there's no such thing as magic, only science."

"Well it would seem that they believe otherwise; but it gets more interesting, let me read you another log."

In an act of desperation, the Alliance sent a high ranking operative to gather Intel on us. His name was Jonathan Flurwick, and we almost killed him as swiftly as the marines sent here before him. That day, The Traveler had been present, and Flurwick was fortunate for it. The Traveler saw the deep

Chiaki asked Tobi to reread the log as there was
so much information to decipher from it. "So, the
Alliance has been sending marines here to die for
some time. That asshole Pearson didn't mention
that," she said, slamming her fist against the wall
behind her.

"Did you follow the part about the marine called
Jonathan Flurwick?" Tobi asked.

"Yeah," she said. "So, he's somehow a descendant
of the people of Yoyvis? And it seems like these
Thundercloaks here on New Yoy are connected to
that Yoyvis planet."

"Indeed, and judging by the logs, Yoyvis is a
planet that was destroyed many years ago. People
fled Yoyvis and ended up on Earth."

"Which means that they must have bred with
humans for many generations," said Chiaki. "Oh my,
Tobi; if all this stuff is true then it could mean that

the first-contact between humans and aliens happened long before meeting the Stowyth's on Mars."

"It could mean many things, Nova. Let me keep searching for data that might be of interest."

"Yeah, you do that," she said, becoming suddenly aware that she was lingering in the corridor for too long.

She walked to the stairway and slowly made her way down, thinking about the weight of these new revelations. This wasn't even the data she had come for and already she had obtained information that could alter history as she knew it.

Below her, the android's footsteps tapped against the floor. Androids were made up of so many materials that it was a challenge to build ones that were light on their feet. Chiaki knew of some private tech companies who had patents for stealth androids, but they weren't affiliated with any particular organization in the Milky Way, meaning that their androids weren't widely distributed.

When Chiaki was halfway down the staircase,

she could see the android from behind. This droid had a smooth olive exterior. It was expensive to build androids that mimicked the appearance of humans or other species, so unless you were the Galactic Alliance—or wealthy—it was likely your android would have a simple color or two-tone design. Droid heads came in many shapes and sizes, this one's resembled a human head except that is was slightly longer at the chin. Its ears pointed at the helix, resembling two antennas at the side of its head. Its fingers were longer than usual. The Thundercloaks had clearly done some modding, but it was all cosmetic. Everything inside the droid was likely the default stock build.

Chiaki's nose wrinkled when she saw how dark it was below. The android would have the advantage here because night vision was so cheap to implement in them that it was pretty much default. Luckily, they couldn't see through walls or solid materials; at least the cheaper models couldn't. The android's head moved left to right as it walked; scanning the area. Chiaki saw an oval shaped room in front of the droid and it aligned correctly with the location of the server room that she'd seen on the infra-red.

She had a small window of opportunity before the android walked back towards the stairway and noticed her, so she crept downstairs until she was on the ground. She found cover against a plain glass wall to her left. She could easily be seen through the glass if she stood, so she knelt in a way that she would be hidden by book shelves inside the room.

Chiaki heard the droid's footsteps coming back down the hallway so she crept around the other side of the wall and continued to move forward; passing the android on the other side of the glass room. If she kept up this this momentum, she could snatch the data from the server room without even needing to shut down the android.

When she was one room away from the oval room, she glanced above her, in search of any cameras or security equipment. It seemed that these Thundercloaks relied heavily on their drones and androids. But Pearson had mentioned that this was an old data center, so it could just be the fact that they'd moved their most expensive security resources to their new facilities.

Chiaki took a glance around the corner to observe the door leading into the oval room. It was a rotating door with tight segments, possibly there to prevent someone from removing large equipment from the room. This worked in Chiaki's favor, because the oval room didn't have glass walls like the other surrounding rooms and the rotating door meant that the droid wouldn't easily be able to see into the room and notice her. The only problem would be going through the rotating doors silently. Rotating doors weren't the quietest method of entering a room. She observed the outside of the room some more, looking for vents, but she couldn't see the other side of the room from where she was knelt. Her options were to either attempt to get through the rotating doors, or sneak past the android again to check for vents on the other side.

Her excitement of the server room being right before her eyes made her impatient and reluctant to backtrack. She would attempt to get through the rotating doors. Once she made it through them, there was a chance the droid would come to investigate the noise; so she would hide somewhere in the room until the coast was clear.

And then, Chiaki's heart skipped a beat as she started to hear the android's footsteps behind her.

CHAPTER NINE

THE ANDROID WAS STILL too far behind to notice Chiaki. It was just cornering the glass room. The android would soon detect her if she didn't make a move.

She dashed forward, making her way towards the rotating door, but in her haste her foot collided with an uneven floor tile, sending her body front ways to the floor. "Shit!" she cried under her breath. The android's footsteps were now fast approaching and in response, Chiaki got up and flattened herself against the wall that it would be emerging next to. She grabbed the SMG and held her breath, waiting for the droid to stray into her sights.

A loud crash came from the direction of the stairway and the android's footsteps came to a halt. Chiaki listened closely for any follow up noises. Unless there were new enemy sentries on the premises, it had to be Vraxen.

The android was moving again, but she could hear that the footsteps were trailing away further from where she stood. It was going to investigate the noise and although Vraxen being discovered could potentially lead to her death, she was thankful for the disturbance.

Chiaki shuffled to the other side of the wall and peered around to see the droid enter the stairwell. She waited a few seconds before dashing towards the oval room and pushing her way through the creaky rotating doors.

Inside, Chiaki took a moment to observe the room. Racks of networking equipment circled the room in a one-hundred-and-eighty degree span. Each rack had around thirty inches of separation. Despite the facility being deserted, the room was cooled, but she heard no air conditioning unit or fans. She looked up and saw a caged vent guard at the center of the roof. The ceiling was domed and it was higher than the ceiling level of the outside hallway.

At the center of the room was a round, erected surface that was a foot smaller than Chiaki was at her incredible height of five-foot four-inches. A computer terminal sat atop the surface. She approached the terminal and circled around it, looking for any security triggers. The terminal's wiring was hidden inside the circular stand, and she could see that the cables ran under the flooring beneath her. She was stood on a mesh strip that housed a number of cables running from the terminal. She followed the cables so that she could locate the equipment that the terminal was connected too. In the worst case scenario, she could pull the cables and shut down any tracking or security software. The many cables branched in different directions, connecting to devices sitting on top of racks at the opposite end of the room.

Chiaki walked back to the terminal and stared at it. It was a display with a fold out keyboard. At the side of the screen there were three ports for external connectivity. Chiaki was thankful that these weren't hidden; it would make her life easier. As she raised her finger to hit the on switch, a call came in on her Comm-link. She held her wrist in front of her and saw Commander Pearson's name blinking on the screen.

She had no reason to speak with him, and more than likely he'd be mad at her for separating from

Vraxen. Besides, he was now interrupting her from doing the task he'd dragged her here for. Of course, there was a chance that he was calling her because of an emergency, but Chiaki figured that if she'd come this far, it wasn't worth stopping now.

She ignored the call and hit the power button on the terminal. There was a catchy jingle from the machines speakers as it kicked into life, and the LED lights all around the room blinked to reflect the terminal powering on. "Wow, I need my bedroom to do that," she said. And then her eyes grew wide with shock when she saw a wall of text pop up on the screen; text that she couldn't understand.

"Tobi," she said, pulling another one of her nifty accessories from her pocket. It was a one-sided eye lens that she could cup over an eye and sync with her Comm-link. It would allow Tobi to process any on-screen information that she was looking at. "Please tell me you know what language this is," she asked.

"Negative. Sorry, Nova, I do not recognize it."

"Hmm, okay, let me try something else then," she pulled the Comm-link cable from its side panel and plugged it into the terminal. "See if you can find a language setting anywhere in the terminal's initializations."

There was silence for around a minute, until Chiaki thought she heard a noise somewhere above, but when no other sounds followed she guessed it must be pests. She started to get impatient by Tobi's lack of communication. "Find anything?"

"I'm sorry, Nova, I'm unable to decipher anything as this language is not recognized.

"Dammit!" she said, ramming her fist on the solid stand. She instantly regretted it and bit her lip to suppress a yelp. She took a deep breath and then thought about what her brother might do in such a situation. No ideas came to mind—after all, it wasn't every day that a hacker came across an unrecognized language—but she remembered something he'd always told her. *No matter how difficult a task appears at first, if it's a piece of hardware, there's always another way to hack it. Sometimes you just have to think outside the box.*

But how much could she think outside the box if she couldn't even get past the first screen? Staring at the screen, she could tell that the terminal was running the Vertex+ operating system, just by the typeface used on the text. Vertex+ was the operating system preferred by any organization that wanted to make it clear they had nothing to do with the Galactic Alliance. No doubt, this version was heavily modified.

She turned around and faced the door, wondering if the android had returned. She'd been so consumed by the thought of getting into the terminal that she forgot the danger that loomed outside the room. She moved forward; squinting her eyes to catch a glimpse of anything moving on the other side of the rotating doors. There was nothing but reflective swirls of the other rooms in the hallway.

And then she remembered. "The library," she said out loud. "There was a library or something. Maybe they have language books in there."

"Good thinking, Nova. It's worth a try."

"Make sure you let me know if you sense Vraxen's frequency, okay?"

"I will."

Chiaki crept out of the server room and pressed her back against the first wall she came to; the same one she'd hidden behind earlier. She listened for any sign of the android's presence. It was too quiet for her liking and she had the uncanny feeling that something was lurking.

After a minute of listening, she crept down the main path of the hall until she came to the glass room with all the book shelves. She pushed her way through the weightless door and looked around the four sides of the small boxed space. She hunched her body low when she realized that her body would be visible over some of the smaller shelves in the room. Even with her short height, the android would have no problem seeing her if it came down the stairs.

She circled around the room, looking up and down each shelf for any sign of a language book. A few times she picked a book from the shelf and flicked through the pages. They were all written in the same weird language that was on the terminal. She could tell it was the same language by the common use of the apostrophe between words.

"There has to be something here that explains this weird language, even if it's written in another language," she said, trying to suppress her voice. A book written in English was preferred, but even if there was a book teaching this mysterious language in one of the other recognized languages, Chiaki would be able to use her Comm-link to translate it. After ten more minutes of losing her patience—in which time she'd started to throw books around the room when they annoyed her—she decided it was time to give up and try to get into the terminal another way. On her way out, her foot knocked one of the books, making it slide against the solid floor. She didn't remember looking at it so she flicked through it until she found a page with instructional text.

Between the many dense paragraphs were segments of text with sequential linebreaks. The linebreaks often came after a specific character was used. "This is definitely a programming language," she said. She could tell by the syntax structure of the words, even though she couldn't understand them. This wouldn't help her get past the terminal screen, but if she could find another way into its source code then this book would come in handy.

Chiaki left the room.

Chiaki was on her way back to the server room when suddenly, a beam of light hit her from behind like a helicopter spotlight. She turned slowly on the spot and saw the android by the stairway with its arm extended; the light beaming from a socket in its arm.

"Ihea ehrae ueao?" it said.

Chiaki was stunned; she would have expected the android to alert its owners already. Instead it was trying to talk to her. "Umm, hello?" she said.

"Oh, you speak English?" the android replied, in a robotic accent she didn't understand. And then something clicked in Chiaki's mind. If the android could speak both English and the mysterious language, it meant that it had a language pack inside its programming. She could use it. "If you can speak English, then it means you shouldn't be here, human."

Suddenly, a red light pulsed inside the androids head. It was sending an alert. "Now, why'd you have to go and do that?" she said, approaching the droid. The machine tried to one up her by dashing towards her and attempting to grab her, but she had the android's movements committed to memory. Chiaki had played around with these things so much that she knew their mechanical limitations, as well as their weak points. When the droid extended its arm to grab her, she used a Wing Chun style block and then put all her weight into a counter punch. The punch connected with the droid's synthetic chest plate and forced him back. Her knuckles ached from the hardness of the metal, but she had no time to let it affect her. She drew the SMG from her side and shot repeatedly into the android's head, shattering a glass panel on its face and shutting down its central processor. The android collapsed in a heap on the floor.

She dragged the android into the library so it wouldn't be in plain sight. "I have to hurry. These Thundercloaks could be on the way here now," she said, as she flipped the machine over so that its face was against the floor.

"With any hope, they're halfway across the planet and won't make it here any time soon," said Tobi.

"That's the best case scenario, but I'm not going

to count on it." She grabbed the robot's hands and pushed back one of its fingers to expose a multi-tool. It was common for androids to have built in screwdrivers so they could carry out self-maintenance when needed. She used the multi tool to unscrew the machine's own back compartment, where the hard drive was kept. After a couple intense minutes of unscrewing, she pulled the harddrive from its back, but didn't take it out all the way. She still needed it to be connected to the machine's power.

"Tobi, you know what to do," she said, connecting her Comm-link to the hard drive. Tobi's swirling icon appeared on the screen to indicate that he was busy running her hacking software. Once he made it past the encryptions on the harddrive, he would then try to locate the language pack, which was considered a plug-in for the android's source code.

After a few more minutes, Tobi's busy symbol faded from the screen. "I've found the language pack, and it has been transferred to your local files."

"Thanks, Tobi," she said, before ripping the harddrive completely from the androids back. She had too much to carry with both the book and the harddrive, but she was keen to hold onto them, at least for now.

Back in the server room, Chiaki reconnected her Comm-link to the terminal. Tobi was now able to read what was written on the screen back to her. He read the large wall of text, which was a checklist of processes running in the facility.

"It's also saying that the alert systems have been activated and that reinforcements have answered the call," said Tobi.

Chiaki couldn't deal with the pressure of a Thundercloak taskforce on its way to wipe her out so she chose to ignore that for now and focus on the hack. "How do we get past the screen?"

"Press the U key," he said. She did as he was told, and then she was presented with a login screen. She looked down at her Comm-link and saw Tobi's swirling icon, which meant that he was already attempting to get past the terminal's security.

"There's a firewall here, we're going to have to get through it," said Tobi.

Chiaki tapped the home screen on her Comm-link and navigated to her file system. She opened up a malware code that she'd written previously, one she was proud of. In order for the malware to work she needed to make some modifications so that it would recognize that the terminal was running the Vertex+ operating system. "Tobi, run Starfade," she said, referring to the malware by its name.

Tobi's swirl blinked on screen and she waited for Starfade to do its magic. The malware would figure out which packets were able to be received by the terminal and clone them, tricking the system into granting access to Chiaki's Comm-link. By the looks of the facility, she guessed that the firewall wasn't updated frequently, meaning it would be easier to exploit.

Her assumptions were proved correctly when Tobi displayed a happy face emoji to her on the Comm-link screen. With the firewall compromised, she could now work on cracking the admin login account. She ran her brute-force cracking software from her Comm-link and watched as it cycled through numerous character combinations in search of the correct ones for both the username and password; this would take some time.

"While we wait, I could read another log from the files we recovered earlier," said Tobi. "With the language pack I am able to decipher much more of them."

"Go for it," Chiaki yawned.

The Traveler is the most fortunate being in the known-universe. He has witnessed many of the wonders of this galaxy and beyond. He was born on Yoyvis among our ancient ancestors, and he was there when they fled the planet before its destruction. He lived on Earth for years, seeing the planets' many marvels; all while going under the radar as not to alert Earth's governments of the presence of galactic refugees. Then, before Relaun was built to cast magic away from the Milky Way, a miracle occurred. The Traveler fell into a time warp, a glitch in the universe if you will. Even The Traveler has no idea how this occurred. He simply followed a strange light presence that had woken him while in the country of Egypt. To his fellow Yoyvis refugees, he had mysteriously disappeared, but according to The Traveler, he'd been stuck in this warp for many generations, with his body and consciousness being preserved in the warp. To him, he was merely asleep for centuries.

And then when the warp faded, he found himself awake in the middle of a horrific war taking place across planets he never knew. Somehow, he'd been transported to a tear inside the galaxy, and he was existing in a new dimension. It took immense survival skills for The Traveler to traverse this mysterious realm, and he suffered many injuries while avoiding both parties involved in the war. Eventually, The Traveler made it back to the Milky Way, and how ironic is it that he came full circle? The Traveler found us, The Children of Yoy, here on New Yoy.

The Children of Yoy founders fled Yoyvis decades before its demise, in secret, to escape its harsh politics. Then, The Traveler and around a hundred more refugees fled decades after to avoid our species being erased from the Milky Way. And now, The Traveler has united with descendants of Yoyvis that he never even knew existed.

The only thing fitting for The Traveler now, would be to make it into Relaun and recover our long-lost powers. Then he could say that he'd seen it all.

"Whoa, am I understating this correctly?" Chiaki asked. "Are you telling me that one of the people who fled Yoyvis for Earth centuries ago is still alive today?" There was so much information to digest from the passage, but this was what stood out to her the most.

"According to the log, yes," said Tobi. "He somehow existed in a time warp, until it eventually faded away."

"What was this new dimension they were talking about?" she asked. Before Tobi could answer that, her Comm-link chimed, indicating that the admin account had been retrieved. "Hold that thought, Tobi."

With the account unlocked, the data she had come for was almost hers for the taking. The terminal displayed a customized graphical-user-interface, but customized or not, Chiaki knew how GUIs worked. After navigating through the strange icons on the desktop, she finally found where the bulk of the terminal's data was stored. She removed the SD card that Pearson had given her and slotted it into her Comm-link. It would be a slower transfer than slotting the card directly into the terminal, but Chiaki wanted to simultaneously clone the data to her own cloud storage. She was sure that Pearson told Vraxen to prevent her using her Comm-link for the transfer, and thus she was glad for ditching him.

Before the transfer could be initiated, a red alert symbol flashed on the terminal's screen. "Nova, it appears that one of the programs on the system is preventing the transfer."

"An extra layer of security, eh?" she said, impressed that these Thundercloaks—or, Children of Yoy—had been smart enough to include additional security measures.

Chiaki clicked the Vertex+ symbol on the keyboard and opened up the system's task manager. With a list of all the programs that were running, she searched through each one that she didn't recognize, until she found the culprit. A program called Stahream was preventing the transfer, so Chiaki opened up the source files.

With the language pack installed, the code was thankfully displaying in English, but Chiaki didn't fully understand the syntax of the code. "Ah ha," she said. "I've got something for you." She picked up the book she had stolen from the library earlier and examined a number of its pages to gain an understanding of the syntax. Here and there, she required Tobi to translate the text with the aid of her eye accessory. After seeing enough of the examples from the book, she soon understood which characters were needed to complete a plausible function in the code.

There was a function in the code preventing data from being transferred to Comm-link devices, so she rewrote the code, using both the book for reference and the many other functions in the source code as a guide. Finally, she saved the re-written code and relaunched the software.

There was now an animated icon on the screen to indicate the data being transferred.

"Nova," Tobi called.

"Yes, dear?"

"Why didn't you try to uninstall the program as admin? It could have worked."

She raised an eyebrow. "Come on, Tobi. How is that fun?"

Chiaki hummed for several minutes, swaying her head and hips side to side in rhythm as she waited for the transfer to complete. It was taking longer because of her desire to clone the data. She soon stopped moving when she heard noises coming from above once more. On inspection, she saw nothing but the caged vent; but considering she'd gone through a vent earlier she knew that anything could be lurking inside.

"Hurry up!" she cried.

And then the caged vent came crashing to the ground behind the terminal. Just as the data transfer had completed, a tall figure fell from the hole in the ceiling and landed on its feet on the other side of the terminal. The figure was human-like, but exceptionally thin. Its eyes had a deep amber shimmer and its skin was a tanned olive shade. But most peculiar of all, its ears pointed upwards like an Elf's would.

Chiaki started to feel a sharp stinging sensation in her left arm. When she tried to pocket Pearson's SD card, she saw that a dagger had pierced through the padding on her skinsuit and opened up a burning gash.

Blood oozed down her arm as her aggressor spoke for the first time. "That was impressive hacking, Earthling, but you will not leave here with that data.”

CHAPTER TEN

CHIAKI'S ARM WAS TORMENTING her more with every passing moment of silence. She wanted nothing more than to remove the dagger, but she knew it would hurt like hell.

She eyed the figure on the other side of the terminal. It wore a brown cloak over its skinsuit and its fingers were full of colorful rings. "Is there a Comic Con on this planet?" she asked. She was trying to convince herself—more than the being in front of her—that she wasn't scared.

It smiled. "You are not with the Alliance are you?" it said, with a voice that was soothing enough to read audiobooks. "But you are here on their behalf."

Chiaki's arm burned, and she started feeling hazy. She assumed that the dagger had hit an artery and she was losing too much blood, and thus, she'd need to tend to it soon. Whatever this species was, she knew it must have fast reflexes to throw the dagger while falling from the ceiling. "What the hell are you?" she asked.

There was a shimmer of amber as it rolled its eyes. "Obviously, I'm one of the Elves from The Children of Yoy. I assumed you were smart enough to come to that conclusion."

She had indeed heard the entries that Tobi had read to her, but never once did she think the idea of Elves existing was a true concept. She thought perhaps that it was a clever title they were using to describe their race. But to see an Elf, looking just like the fictional depictions of them from Earth was too far-fetched for her to process.

"Next thing you'll tell me is that Santa banished you from the North Pole," she said; her head foggy.

"Let me guess...an Earth joke? Your people have been committing the Elves from Yoyvis to legend for centuries. After the Yoyvis refugees were seen, your ancestors on Earth passed down stories of us, until they became symbolic in your literature. And now I hear we're popular in your visual entertainment too." The Elf's hand swayed as he talked. "Well, we are not to be romanticized, Ahnaf. And you should know that there is poison from that dagger working its way through your system. You'll be dead within the next hour."

No wonder it's burning so much—she thought. *Who the heck even poisons people these days?*

"Nova, I am reading a blueprint file of this building," said Tobi in her ear. "I will let you know if I find a suitable means of escape."

Chiaki knew she needed to take some action here if she wanted to live, and she hoped Tobi would find something useful, like a secret door right below her feet. In the meantime, she needed to keep the Elf talking while she thought of a backup plan. "So...all of the people from Yoyvis and you guys here on New Yoy are Elvish?"

"The term we prefer is Elven. And no, Yoyvis was home to both Elven people and Ahnaf people. The Ahnaf are biologically identical to you. They are what you call, human."

"I guess that makes sense why there's an Alliance marine from Earth related to you people," she said.

"Perhaps, but Elves can also interbreed with humans." he smiled. "But I'm not suggesting that the marine is a mixed breed, of course.”

“Nova!” came Tobi’s voice, “at the back of the room, behind the Elf, there is a ladder near one of the racks that leads to a trapdoor on a higher level. The lock is already disengaged.”

How am I going to get behind the Elf and climb up a ladder without it coming after me? She was unable to respond to Tobi without the Elf knowing the context of her conversation, so she thought her response instead. Too bad Tobi couldn’t hear her thoughts.

“Look, Yoy Boy, here’s the thing; I don’t give a shit about the Galactic Alliance or this data. Could you please give me some kind of potion to cure this and let me get out of your way?”

The Elves’ fingers swayed before him, and then she saw a small blade expose itself over its fingers, as if the blade had emerged from his palm. “I can’t let you leave here with the knowledge you’ve obtained.”

With her non-poisoned arm, Chiaki positioned her hand in a way that she’d be ready to grab her SMG. “But you just spent like five minutes giving me *said* knowledge.”

"Yes; knowledge that will die with you."

The burning sensation was working its way up the entirety of her arm now. She knew she was running low on time. "Well..." she said, before faking a fit of coughs. "Since this is my last hour, how about you tell me your name; maybe I'll remember it in the afterlife."

The Elf kept that same stupid, smug smile on his face. "The name is Rozzar. But..."

Chiaki held up the SMG and shot a barrage of bullets at Rozzar. His reflexes were so fast that he was able to deflect the bullets with his dagger. She stopped firing, with the worry that the shots would rebound back at her.

Now flustered, she ran around the terminal and swung her leg into the air, trying to catch his head. Again, Rozzar dodged her, and the two played a game of dodging punches and kicks. Chiaki was able to dip low and retrieve her hidden blade from a pocket on her shin. When she rose she swung the blade up to Rozzar with her right arm; but Rozzar was way too fast, and was able to knock the blade from her hand with a backhand.

And then; Rozzar slammed his knee into her infected arm. Chiaki realized that she was at a severe disadvantage and began shooting glances in the direction of the ladder. Rozzar's kick had intensified the burning in her arm and she needed to escape now.

He stood there, with the dagger at his tips. She waited for him to make a move on her, but she could tell that like her, Rozzar was a defensive fighter. He preferred to wait until his foe made a move he could counter. Chiaki became impatient and flicked her thumb over the lock on her SMG, before tossing it at Rozzar, forcing him to dodge it. She used the short distraction to run to the back of the room. She kicked a cabinet on wheels into the path behind her, desperate to cause obstruction. But just as she saw the gunmetal ladder steps that were bound to the wall, she felt Rozzar's arms lock around her neck.

She didn't know what she was thinking. In fact, she wasn't thinking at all when she threw her weapon away. Perhaps the poison was slowly making its way to her brain. She felt sharp pain as Rozzar pulled the blade from her arm. He then dangled it in front of her chest.

There was some kind of crashing sound behind them. Perhaps it was the cabinet tipping over after Rozzar had brushed passed it at his super Elf speed.

She knew it was a bad idea to take this stupid job and now she could only hope that her people on Flade would be left alone once Pearson's mission had failed. At least she would see her brother again.

Suddenly, Chiaki felt the Elf release her and she suffered from a spell of dizziness as she staggered on her feet. She went completely deaf for a few seconds, and couldn't register what was happening around her.

Slowly, her vision returned and she saw Vraxen trading blows with Rozzar. Watching him save her life filled her with guilt for ditching him.

Rozzar, in true show-off form had flipped backwards a few times to create some space between them. From across the room, Vraxen extended his arm and grabbed the Elf by the collar; he then lifted him into the air so that his body dangled in Vraxen's hands. For the first time, Rozzar's face showed panic, like he wasn't in control anymore.

But then Chiaki saw that Rozzar was holding the dagger that he'd pulled from her arm. "Watch out!" she cried. Rozzar stabbed Vraxen in the arm and Vraxen responded by hurling Rozzar across the room so that he collided with a rack of hardware. His body was curled up on the floor with his cloak blanketing him.

When Vraxen made it over to her, he lifted her from her feet and rested her on a nearby table.

"Vraxen, your arm," she said. "It's probably poisoned."

"Hm," he grunted. She watched him pull the knife from his graphite skin and a thick blue substance dripped from it. He then poked the gash with his finger, and in doing so he grunted a few more times. And then, with thick blue goo over two of his fingers, Vraxen pressed them over Chiaki's arm. She yelped at the stinging sensation and then took a sharp intake of breath to stop herself from screaming. Vraxen pressed his rough fingers against the wound and it felt like he was trying to push as much of his goo into her as possible.

"Stowyth blood is immune from most poisons, and it has healing properties when used on humans. This may not get rid of the poison in your body because it's been in there too long, but hopefully it will slow it long enough for us to get out of here and get you some help."

It took Chiaki several moments of huffing and puffing before she could respond. "Thank you," she said.

"Did you get the data?"

"Yes, I have it," she replied.

She saw Vraxen typing on his Comm-link. "She has the data, Pearson. We need extraction now, and fast."

Chiaki sat herself up, feeling somewhat better. But she didn't know how much longer she had, even with Vraxen's blood helping her. "That asshole, Pearson," she said. "He knew that the people on this planet had been killing Alliance Marines for years, yet he sends me and you here to do their dirty work. Probably so he won't have to deal with more Alliance paperwork if we die."

"Nevermind that now," said Vraxen, helping her

off the table.

Now back on her feet, Chiaki looked over where Rozzar's body was but it had disappeared. "Oh shit."

"Watch out!" Vraxen cried as he extended his arm and pushed Chiaki out the way of Rozzar, who had been swinging a dagger at them from behind. The dagger had struck Vraxen's arm once more, and drops of the glowing, blue goo dripped on the floor.

The two of them continued to trade blows, with Rozzar being able to dodge a majority of Vraxen's wide swings. Chiaki tried to think of a way to assist, but she still didn't have full use of her arm. It felt stiff to move, and she could feel stinging throbs inside.

She slowly moved around the brawl, in search of her SMG. She had just located the weapon when she was blindsided by a blow to her back. She fell on her injured arm, maximizing the pain. When she looked up she saw Rozzar leaning in to grab her, but she responded by sweeping her leg around, making her foot connect with the side of his head. Rozzar staggered from the blow and Chiaki looked around for Vraxen. She saw that he was on his knees behind Rozzar, with one arm leaning against a rack of hardware.

Rozzar—clearly prioritizing Chiaki because of the data—approached her once he'd recovered. She continued to kick at him but he caught her by the foot and yanked her whole body towards him. Rozzar lifted her by her neck and held her high above his head. Chiaki could feel her supply of oxygen closing as he applied more and more pressure.

From behind Rozzar, Vraxen's arm reached for the SMG. Once he'd grabbed it, he extended his arm to Chiaki so she could grab it from right behind Rozzar's head. Rozzar's amber irises registered that her weapon had been handed to her, but it was too late. Chiaki flicked her thumb over the lock and then aimed the SMG down at the Elf's chest before opening fire. She didn't let the trigger go until she felt her body slam against the ground.

Chiaki had blacked out. When consciousness returned to her, she realized that she was folded over Vraxen's shoulder. She heard his loud footsteps rapping against a metal surface. She opened her eyes and saw they were on the platform where they had entered the building earlier, but Chiaki saw Vraxen run past the corner leading to the main entrance.

"Where are you going?" she said.

"Oh, Nova, you're awake," he said. "There is an elevator that goes up to the roof on the opposite side of this platform. It was non-functional earlier, but now it has a light on. Do you see it," he said, pointing.

Chiaki had to use the little strength she had in her body to raise her neck enough to see where he was pointing. "Yes," she said. "I think Tobi may have activated it once I obtained access to the server."

"Tobi?"

"My personal A.I."

"That explains it then. I think the building will soon be surrounded by the Thundercloaks, so it would be too dangerous for a ground level extraction. Pearson will meet us on the roof."

"Children of Yoy is what they call themselves. I refuse to use any name that lameass Pearson came up with."

"Explain later," said Vraxen, as he walked around a corner of the platform.

"Nova, the drone outside is picking up movement," said Tobi. "I'm showing you the camera now."

She edged her injured arm up in front of her face and felt sharp pain. She stared at her Comm-link screen and saw a number of ground vehicles pulling up outside the front door. "They're coming, Vraxen, the drone alerted me. Let me down please."

"We're almost at the elevator," he said. "And you're not well, remember?"

"I know, just let me down. I want to be able to defend myself if they catch up."

Vraxen obliged and carefully set her down on her feet. He then removed her SMG from a strap on his waist and handed it to her, before removing his assault rifle. The rife had been folded up to make it easier to carry. Vraxen unfolded it and locked it in position. He then took a clip from his belt and inserted it at the bottom of the rifle. Chiaki knew the clip in her SMG was low so she attempted to reload her own weapon, but her stiff arm made it difficult.

Vraxen took the clip from her and slapped it into the SMG on her behalf.

Then they heard a loud sizzling sound coming from the main entrance. Sparks were dripping from the door and a large slit was making its way down. Because Chiaki had rewritten the biometric authentication, they were unable to gain access through the door. It seemed they'd resorted to cutting a hole through it.

"Come," said Vraxen, reaching for her arm.

"Ouch, watch it," she said.

"I'm sorry. Come quickly." The two of them ran to the elevator, and Chiaki felt her head weave as she tried to force her legs to work. As Vraxen slammed his fist against the button to call the elevator, they heard a crash come from the main door. The Children of Yoy reinforcements were now in the building.

The elevator doors opened and the two of them stepped inside. Vraxen immediately hit the button to take them to the roof and while they waited for the doors to close they saw over a dozen cloaked figures run along the platform across from them. Chiaki noted that there were both Elves and humans, but mainly Elves. Some of them were beginning to open fire so Chiaki ducked, while Vraxen opted to return fire. Luckily, the closing doors ate most of the exchange.

They were now shut inside the elevator and it took thirty seconds before they felt themselves moving. Chiaki's body now felt too heavy for her to try and get back up on her feet so she shifted her weight to her buttocks and stayed on the ground.

"Hold on just a little longer. We're almost out of here."

She looked up at Vraxen and nodded, feeling too exhausted to speak.

"Nova!" Tobi called in her ear, "we've lost connection to the drone; it's been destroyed."

"Shit!" she slurred. "There are more of them outside. Let's just hope they don't mess with extraction." She looked up at Vraxen to make it clear she was talking to him. "Call your boss and see what the ETA is."

Vraxen complied, and she heard him speak with Pearson a few seconds later. "Pearson, what's the

ETA on extraction?" Chiaki couldn't hear what the response from Pearson was. "Yes, we're aware of them. Just make your way here as quick as possible and we'll hold them off as best we can in the meantime. Please also have a medic at the ready to treat Nova for poison." She appreciated his regard for her predicament.

"Pearson says he's three minutes away, and he saw a Thundercloak shuttle nearby our location."

"Oh, so Goldilocks is making an appearance himself, eh?"

The elevator chimed and a light on the panel blinked to indicate they had reached the roof. Vraxen held his hand out to Chiaki and she grabbed it with her right arm. She pulled herself up with difficulty and stumbled to her feet. When the door opened they saw a flat and wide surface with railings surrounding the area. Aside from the bolts of lightning rippling through the air and the sounds of thunder that followed, it was a little too quiet.

"Nova, once we see the shuttle come into view, I need you to climb on my back, throw your bad arm around my neck for support if you can. And then try to use your good arm to fire at the Thundercloaks, okay?"

She nodded.

"I will do the best I can to make a run for it," Vraxen continued. The light on the elevator blinked, indicating that it was being called below. Vraxen grabbed Chiaki by her good hand and led her through the doors, holding his rifle up cautiously as he did so. Chiaki looked around for any sign of the Yoy, but her vision blurred each time her head swiveled.

"Look." Vraxen whispered. She followed his line of sight and saw the Astrid descending through the sky. At the moment that relief started to fill inside her, a number of figures stepped into her peripheral vision from both sides. She looked left to right and saw a dozen cloaked individuals aiming blasters, different from the ones they'd seen downstairs.

"Remember what I said," Vraxen told her under his breath. He tossed his rifle on the floor in front of him and held his arms in the air. He then lowered himself as if submitting to the Children of Yoy. Chiaki moved her bad arm to see how much difficulty she would have holding onto Vraxen.

In the distance, the shuttle was moving closer to the roof and some of the cloaked individuals started opening fire in its direction. Within seconds, the Astrid was returning fire, causing them to break formation and scatter to find cover behind generators.

"Now!" Vraxen yelled. Chiaki pushed herself onto his back and swung her bad arm around his neck. The pain was so bad that tears fell down her cheeks as she groaned. She felt Vraxen rise to his feet and he hooked one of her legs under his arm. She felt more discomfort as Vraxen began sprinting, as the hardness of his body knocked against her.

She had motion blur in her eyes as the Stowyth continued to sprint, but she could see red beams flying all around them. When she chanced a look behind, she saw way too many of the Yoy aiming weapons their way, the sight made her scared for her life.

She drew the SMG from her leg that dangled freely behind Vraxen's back and she fired a barrage of shots behind her, not paying too much attention to where she was aiming. She just wanted to make them take cover so there would be less chance of them getting a lucky shot.

Soon enough, the Astrid's engines could be heard. When Chiaki peered over Vraxen's shoulder she saw Commander Pearson poking out the side door; firing somewhere behind them.

"Send her up!" she heard Pearson say once his gun had gone silent.

She felt Vraxen get low on his knees again. "Nova, climb up," he said.

Through her blurred vision, she could see Pearson's arm reaching for her above. She holstered the SMG again and then yelped as she moved her other arm from around Vraxen's neck. Then she shuffled herself up his back, stepping on his shoulder to close the gap between them and the Astrid. She raised her good arm up and Pearson grabbed it.

Chiaki screamed as Pearson yanked her up into the Astrid with no consideration for her pain. "Where's the data?" he asked right away.

"Vraxen," she responded.

"First give me the data. It's what we came for."

She didn't want to hand it over so soon, but in

the moment she was only concerned for Vraxen's safety. Vraxen had looked out for her, even after she'd been so bitter towards him. She went into the pocket she had the SD card stashed in and tossed it onto the ground next to her. Only then did she register another person inside the Astrid with white rubber gloves. A medic she hoped.

While Pearson scrambled for the data, Chiaki tried to sit herself up to help Vraxen. He had arms that could extend; why was he taking so long to join them? When she peered outside she had her answer.

The cloaked hecklers had surrounded them and some of them were now beginning to fire directly at the Astrid. Without his weapon, Vraxen had to use his extending arms to knock them back one by one. But he was taking heavy fire and soon enough the beams would penetrate his exterior.

Pearson leaned out and fired down on the cloaked menaces, taking a few of them out. But then, they saw more of them flooding out from the elevator in the distance. "There's too many of them. We have the data, let's get out of here."

"No!" Chiaki cried. "Get Vraxen, he's right

there."

"We'll come back for him shortly. I just need time to upload the data without the Astrid getting wrecked."

The Astrid door began to close and in a fit of rage, Chiaki attempted to grab her SMG. But that was the exact moment that her body shut down and she faded away.

CHAPTER ELEVEN

"HOW'S IT GOING, DOC?" asked Pearson.

"So far so good; there's a high probability she will survive. The Stowyth did well to give his blood to her. It stopped the poison from spreading through her entire system. Some of the poison did flow past her arm, which is why she passed out. Her body needed to shut down to try and make sense of the chemical and fight it. Luckily, through surgery I was able to flush out what little poison had spread past the arm."

"Excellent," said Pearson. "She did us a great deed so she at least deserves another shot at life."

"Yes. But the problem is that her arm is too badly damaged. Once the effects of the Stowyth blood wear off, the poison will spread again. And it's not as easy as flushing it out. There's already longterm damage."

"How far into her arm is it?" Pearson asked. The doctor slid his arm above her bicep, indicating the area. "Can you amputate her?" Pearson asked.

"There's a chance we could keep her in this state long enough for us to find a remedy back at base," said the doctor. "There may still be longterm damage, but if we find a remedy she could keep her arm."

"Screw that, I don't want her there. Just amputate her."

The heart monitor beeped frantically.

"What's wrong?" Pearson asked.

The doctor felt his patients' pulse and then used a finger to lift her left eyelid. "Oh my; she's conscious. She can hear us."

"Knock her out again and carry out the procedure as soon as possible."

The doctor walked across the room to get his Anesthesia.

CHAPTER TWELVE

- 3 Weeks Later -

THE SIMULATION ROOM WAS a gymnasium sized area where hackers could set challenges for comrades who wanted to test their skills. Recently, the area had gone completely forgotten. There were thirty-one total residents on the tiny planet of Flade and they were so confident in one another's abilities that there was rarely anything to prove. Any freelance work that came through the shared inbox was often so straightforward that real skills were hardly required.

Chiaki always tried to persuade her friends to prepare for advances in technology and new programming libraries that were being introduced but it was hard to keep them motivated when there was never a need to practice. As a result, most of the team spent countless hours playing virtual reality simulators and massively multi-player games. At times when they were struggling to pay for taxes and planet rights for Flade, they would actively search for new clientele.

Today was different for Chiaki. Upon waking, Chiaki had asked her closest friend, Sage, to prepare a simulation for her. Sage's real name was Lilian Ross, and she was a fellow lone-child from Earth. Lilian was abandoned by her real parents as a baby because they'd dropped everything to travel around the Milky Way together, which was an expensive thing to do. Ship fuel didn't come cheap, and that was especially true twenty-something years ago. Unlike Chiaki, Lilian's parents could be still alive in the Milky Way somewhere; she just didn't know where they were or what they were calling themselves now. When recruiting new residents, Chiaki always had a preference for orphaned hackers.

Chiaki had asked Sage to rig the simulation room with the most complex obstacles she could come up with; because tonight would be the night that she set out to get answers. Sage had pleaded with Chiaki to let it go.

"Look, Nova," she'd said. "I know how hot-headed you can be. And I know you're still pissed at those douche-bags for holding us hostage and using you. But you only lost an arm three weeks ago, and I don't care if you've replaced it with a synthetic arm, your body still needs time to recover. And you need to adapt to the change. It's a traumatic thing to lose an arm you know; even if you do have a bionic one."

Chiaki had enjoyed the process of securing herself a new arm. AMG systems was an official artillery manufacturer for the Galactic Alliance; they owned a smaller R&D company called Sparse Manufacturing. Sparse specialized in creating products that only the most elite Alliance officials would gain access to. After doing some research on synthetic arms, Chiaki had found a press release from three years prior that detailed a limited edition synthetic arm that came with a socket that needed to be permanently plugged into the owners' neurons. After a few hours, Chiaki had hacked into Sparse's network and she saw that one of the final five units of the left-arm version had been ordered and was set to be delivered. Chiaki had updated the delivery location to an exchange station.

At an exchange station, people could have things delivered there and fly in to pick it up at their own convenience. A perfect service if someone didn't want a record of delivery on their home planet. One of Chiaki's comrades who lived on Flade had gone to pick up the arm for her, and he'd made sure to erase any record of the product arriving and leaving the exchange from their database. She could just imagine some overpaid Alliance official waiting patiently for his arm. Perhaps he'd already paid for a new one. Because what was three million credits to a high ranking Alliance official?

The synthetic arm was the reason Chiaki had needed a session in the simulation room. She needed to test the arm out in real situations.

Chiaki was tired of sitting around on Flade while Commander Pearson was walking around with the Intel she had stolen for him. And the asshole didn't even have the decency to tell her what he knew about her brother's murder like he'd promised.

Chiaki couldn't stand clients that didn't pay on the back-end. She'd always dealt with them by exposing their secrets, or stealing from them. Pearson hadn't been a client officially, but he'd disregarded their verbal agreement. He was also responsible for her loss of a limb. And furthermore, Pearson abandoned his own mercenary after he'd saved Chiaki's life. Chiaki had tried to make contact with Vraxen when she'd regained consciousness on Flade, but there was never any response. She feared the worst. She'd even gone to the extent of doing some digging in the database of a popular Utrion discussion board. She'd learned that one of the loan sharks on Utrion still had an outstanding hit on Vraxen. There was an order to kill Vraxen on sight; should he ever show his face in Utrion again. This suggested that Pearson had not paid off the loan shark. For Pearson's violations, Chiaki would make him pay handsomely.

But for now, her plan was to sneak into one of the Galactic Alliance data stations that Tobi had learned about while she was on the Lapwing. She would search for all known Intel on her brother's murder, because she couldn't rest any longer without learning what Pearson knew.

But also, the Intel she'd stolen for Pearson on

New Yoy was too juicy for her to ignore. Much of the data had been diagnostics, blueprints and surveillance footage. There were many documents that Chiaki couldn't make sense of. But one piece of text in particular stood out as the piece of Intel that Pearson was after.

My lover was stolen from me and my heart will never beat as it once did. Ailmon committed treachery with the Alliance soldier that turned out to have Yoyvis genes. It was The Traveler himself that accepted Flurwick as family, despite the fact that we Children of Yoy consider ourselves separate from the immigrants of Yoyvis. But The Traveler's reasons were selfish.

The Traveler was prepared to enter Relaun and recover the Celestibus. Doing so would allow us to cast the magic we've been deprived of for generations. But Ailmon, my love, was against magic being part of the Milky Way again. He wanted things to remain as they were on New Yoy. The thought of magic awakening in thousands of beings around the galaxy was a frightening one. For if Flurwick himself was identified as a descendant of Yoyvis, imagine how many more there are out there. Desperate to prevent a potential war for power in the Milky Way, Ailmon approached Flurwick and told him about the Death Shard.

The Traveler himself told us all about the Death Shard, and swore us to secrecy. The magic energy that comes from the Celestibus causes crystals to form all across the lands where the energy resides. This happened on Yoyvis, and The Traveler told us it would be the case in Relaun too. The people of Yoyvis were always forbidden to harness the powers of the Death Shard, because not only does it allow the most powerful sorcerers to kill with a wave of the hand, but it also enables the gift of absorption.

According to The Traveler, there was a prophecy on Yoyvis about a sorcerer being so powerful that he's able to use the Death Shard to absorb the Celestibus from the heart of the planet and become the only being able to harness magic in the galaxy.

Ailmon told Flurwick this theory. And then Flurwick made it his goal to become the sorcerer that was prophesied. Flurwick went as far as to hunt down ancient scrolls from our ancestors to prove this theory correct. And then, when The Traveler offered Flurwick the task of entering Relaun to recover the Celestibus, he happily obliged, but for his own greed.

But just a day after Flurwick entered Relaun, The Traveler

had an unsettling feeling about him. "I don't know if we should be so trusting of an Alliance marine," he'd said. I considered him a fool for waiting until it was too late to express these concerns.

He visited me at my data center and asked me to roll back every video and audio log that had captured Flurwick during his days here. It was then that we saw the footage of Ailmon corresponding with Flurwick and telling him about the Death Shard. Shortly after, I found my lover with his throat slit. And then all security operations were moved away from my data center.

I write this so that one day it will be understood why I have isolated myself from the pack. Should I meet my demise, this will be evidence of the events that transpired.

- Rozzar

Back on New Yoy, Chiaki had been too consumed with the mission to process what the logs had meant. But after having weeks to adjust to her missing limb—in which time she'd suffered extreme phases of depression—she'd been able to re-read the entries hundreds of times.

It was difficult to fathom the fact that an ancient race of Elves and humans—existing over a thousand years before first-contact with the Stowyths in 2033—had been using magic. They'd deemed this magic too dangerous and had casted it away into another world and then colonized it. And now, an Alliance marine with Yoyvis DNA had entered the magical world of Relaun to restore magic back to the Milky Way. But this Flurwick character had gone rogue. Not only had he betrayed the trust of the Children of Yoy, but Chiaki suspected that he was also acting against the wishes of the Galactic Alliance. In which case, she didn't blame him.

If everything she read was real, she knew a shit-storm was brewing in the galaxy. She had to learn more about what the Galactic Alliance was doing about this conspiracy. Being a gamer, she was partly excited by the idea of Elves and magic, but she wondered if this whole ordeal might be some crazy hoax.

"Looks like I should have made the simulation more complicated," said Sage, as Chiaki sat daydreaming after her session. "I went easy on you because of the arm."

"Don't ever go easy on me."

Chiaki had destroyed three drones and dismantled an android during the simulation. All of that in addition to hacking a network that Sage had rigged to set off Chiaki's shock vest if she was detected. She'd passed the simulation with flying colors, but she was still finding it difficult to adjust to the added weight of the arm.

The arm had some incredible features though. It had a dark metallic finish that went from the socket down to its fingertips, but Chiaki modded it so that she could clip on custom claws of any color she desired. Currently she favored purple claws.

A circle at the middle of her palm could open up, to fire small mechanical orbs. For instance, she could now fire her mini-EMPs directly from her palm, making drone tackling even fancier. The arm had ripples circling down the forearm, stopping at the wrist. Inside the ripples, much of the technical functionality was housed. There was a multi-tool inside one of her fingers, and she could also fuse cables together inside her knuckles.

Best of all, she no longer had to wear a Comm-link, because the arm featured holographic Comm-link software that would project a screen above the arm on command. The holographic screen would respond to either Chiaki's voice commands or the fingerprints from her right hand. She'd already migrated all her data from her old Comm-link to the arm, including Tobi. Perhaps one of Chiaki's most celebrated features was the ability to record hand and finger movements as macros. This was particularly useful when applying her makeup or braiding her hair.

Flade's doctor—by default—was a male of the Garrue species who went by the nickname, Lanxton. Garrues were reptile-like humanoids that were revered in the Milky Way for their smarts. It was Lanxton that had carried out the procedure of fusing the arm's socket into Chiaki's neurons. This made it so that the arm really was an extension of her mind. This wasn't just a prosthetic arm that could be used to help her grab cans of soda.

✻ ✻ ✻

"Why won't you let any of us come with you, Nova?" asked Sage.

"How many times do I have to tell you?" Chiaki yelled, as she threw bags of her things into the Yamata. The Yamata was one of two spacecrafts that resided on Flade, and it was primarily flown by Chiaki herself. "I don't want anyone else here mixed up in this Alliance crap. They have free reign over the Milky Way, which makes them dangerous. I'm not involving anyone else here in this."

"We're involved just by association," Sage responded.

"That's true, but I need you all to stay here and protect the planet. If you don't hear from me for a week straight then clip up and be ready for the worst. Maybe even think about fleeing."

"You're so stubborn," said Sage.

Chiaki registered the look of distaste that Sage carried on her face. She noted the hot pants she wore, with the plaid shirt hanging from shoulder to waist line. She noted Sage's sandals, revealing chipped nail polish. Sage was not prepared to leave with Chiaki. If it had been Chiaki in Sage's position, she would have dressed accordingly and forced her way onto the Yamata, no questions asked. Sage didn't want this at all. She only wished for their lives to carry on as normal; and Chiaki's desire to get even with Pearson meant a possible disruption to the usual flow of things on Flade.

"You're damned right I'm stubborn," she finally responded. "To me, hacking isn't just sitting at the computer phishing passwords and writing keyloggers. Sometimes we gotta do what we gotta do to change the galaxy for the better." It was another quote from her brother. "Look after everyone for me," she said finally, before walking up the slope and into the ship.

CHAPTER THIRTEEN

STATION SIXTY, WAS A GALACTIC ALLIANCE space station that was fourteen Earth hours away from the The Kuiper Belt. It had taken Chiaki two and a half days to travel to the station from Flade using her level two FTL. Station Sixty was mostly used as a data center, but they were smart enough not to advertise this fact, because there would always be hackers as rash as Chiaki willing to try their luck.

From observation, security mostly consisted of high-end drones and androids. These ones were more deadly than the ones that had been on New Yoy, by far. And they were programmed to shoot intruders first and ask questions later. There was also a unit of marines of different species living on-site. According to what Tobi had found online, a new unit was assigned this detail every six months.

To make it onto Station Sixty, Chiaki had left the Yamata stationary in orbit, because trying to dock her ship would be the fastest way to a prison cell on

Trador. She'd taken a shuttle closer to the station, equipped her breather and used a Jet Booster to glide her way onto the station. She'd used a few of her gadgets to detect cameras and other security equipment on her way in.

She now stood outside one of many doors. Station Sixty was like a giant disk surrounded by six mini disks. Each of the mini buildings had a long concourse pathway connecting it to the central building. Each of the mini buildings were referred to as nodes. Chiaki was currently on node four.

She had considered landing beside the main building, as that was the most logical place to find the mainframe; but it would also have the tightest security. She figured it would be easier to try her luck entering from one of the nodes and navigating the concourse. It would allow her to scout the main building.

The door leading into node four was secured with a combination of biometrics and a scanner that would verify a marines' access. Chiaki could have tried to crack the door in the usual way, but she wanted to try something else.

"Time to put this arm to the test." She raised her new arm and balled the fingers into a fist to strike a pose of dominance. She then walked closer to the door, but the weight of the arm almost put her off balance. "Damn, I gotta get used to this."

She paced around, looking for the doors' cabling. With this being such a high-end station, the cabling was hidden from sight. She just needed to find a small gap in the wall that would give away where some of the cables were housed. After keeling down, she noticed a small chipped crevice beside the bottom of the door.

"Ah ha," she said. She flicked her synthetic little-finger to activate a flashlight. The light from her finger revealed tiny gaps in the surface. "Looks like this entire panel opens up; there's probably a tool that opens it. I just need to find where it's locked."

Chiaki located the point where the panel opened up after crawling along the bottom of the wall for a few feet. "Tobi, play some Nujabes," she said. "I need some background music to kill this awful silence." As the jazzhop sounds bled into her earpiece, she lifted the cap on her index finger—which had one of her purple claws attached—and using her nerve endings she was able to make a multi-tool slide up from the finger. She selected the tool she needed and popped the panel open.

"You're enjoying this, aren't you?" said Tobi in her earpiece. She was also wearing her eyepiece, so Tobi had a clear view of everything she was doing.

"Duh! I lost an important part of the human body, you know. I gotta at least enjoy my overpowered bionic arm as compensation."

A thick cable ran along the bottom of the wall, going much further around the building than the length of the panel she had just opened. But Chiaki wouldn't need to go any further than where she was. Using one of the other tools in her finger, she sliced the cable open. The security system attached to the door let off a loud horn sound to indicate that it had gone offline. Luckily, it wasn't loud enough to alert anyone; but if someone happened to be watching a live feed of all Station Sixty's security devices, they might notice that that it was now offline. She had to be quick.

Chiaki made the multi-tool slide back into her

finger and she sealed the top of it again. One of the other useful features of the arm was the ability to hook cables into her knuckles. This allowed for the arm to become a temporary adapter, and with her built-in holographic Comm-link, the possibilities would be endless for a hacker.

She fed one side of the cable into the end of her knuckle that her index finger was attached to, and the other end of the cable at the opposite side. A light pulsated from the inside of her forearm to indicate that a signal was found.

"Tohato," she said. It was the word she had set to quickly launch the holographic Comm-link. The word happened to be her favorite Japanese snack. The holographic screen beamed up from her wrist, stopping a few inches from her face. "Align vertical," she said, telling the Comm-link to display vertically along her arm. Keeping the cables in place meant that she couldn't bend her arm to use the Comm-link as usual.

She used her organic hand to navigate the Comm-link and access the door's signal through the cables. It took her three minutes to mess with the doors' binary and activate the opening mechanism. Soon, she had successfully bypassed the security system and the doors shot open.

Now, if Chiaki simply removed the cables from her knuckles, the door would be stuck open and would be unable to shut. She needed to be able to shut it once she got inside to cover her tracks. Thankfully, the arm also had a nifty cable fusing feature.

After typing in the settings on her Comm-link she heard the fusion taking place at the top of her palm. A green icon blinked on the Comm-link screen when the procedure was complete and then she arced her wrist down to pull a panel open at the top of her synthetic palm. She removed the cable that was now fused together and placed it back into the wall. She put her palm back together and got up on her feet.

"Tobi, stop the music now," she said. Concentration would now be needed.

Chiaki had made her way to the main disk of Station Sixty. Sneaking her way through node four and past the concourse had been light-work. She'd encountered drones along the way and she'd dealt with them by firing mini-EMP balls from her palm. After hacking one of the drones, she'd been able to see the locations of all other drones in the facility, and she'd done her best to avoid their paths. She'd also learned that four androids spent their entire day walking through all nodes, and that their patterns were rescheduled each day. She hadn't been able to find any Intel on the locations of the marines on the premises, but she was sure they'd be lurking somewhere in the main building.

Chiaki was pressed against the wall, under a security camera, staying out of its line of sight. She observed her surroundings closely, looking for any obstacles or hidden traps. A security android was scheduled to walk through here in twenty-five minutes. It would circle the entire floor, enter every room and continue up the building, repeating its inspection across all six floors.

The area Chiaki stood in was a wide cylinder lobby, allowing her to peer through the windows of three large areas. One was a kitchen, one was a room full of computers, one a conference room and there was a fourth room that was completely walled off, preventing her from seeing into it. Looking up to the floor above, she could see cabling running vertically up the walls. With this, she guessed that the mainframe was on the top floor. At the center of the lobby was a solid white pole that went all the way up to the roof of the building. Railings connected to the pole on each floor.

The camera above her turned at ten second intervals, covering three directions: left, forward, right. Chiaki waited until it had just faced the direction on the right before she crept left and found the stairway going up.

Twenty minutes later, Chiaki had made her way up to the sixth floor undetected. She'd also located the mainframe, which was inside a dark room full of technical equipment; similar to the sever room she'd visited in New Yoy.

Chiaki was immediately on edge from the darkness upon entering its twin white doors. The server room back on Yoy had had enough lighting to take the edge off, but here she felt like an evil darkness was swallowing her. She called for her Comm-link and activated the light strips built into her skinsuit. She had them set to the same shade of purple as her claws, but she decided to change them to a lime-green hue that would allow more light to bounce around the room.

She located the mainframe terminal and connected the retractable cable that was stowed on the side of her shiny new arm. She went to work taking down the network's security; using Starfade to penetrate firewalls.

"Man, you'd think this would be more difficult to hack into than some random data center on an uncharted world," she said.

"True, but you do have most of the tools needed to hack English language systems already," said Tobi. "Not all hackers come prepared with pre-written code I'm sure."

"Are you saying I'm great, Tobi? Because it sure sounds like that," she smiled.

When she'd bypassed all of the terminal's security, she stared at the screen for a few seconds.

This was it, the moment where she might finally learn the truth. She hoped that the answers would be here, and that she wouldn't need to find another Alliance data center. She opened up a search window, opting to use her Comm-link to control the interface. She then typed her brother's name...

Kura Nakayama

A small animated magnifying glass indicated that the system was searching for any and all data that held the name. All kinds of intelligence documents popped up, from identification records to his planetary lease of Flade—which was now in her name. Chiaki even saw her own records popping up.

"Jeez, no matter how hard I work to scrub all records of myself from existence, they always find a way to gather more data."

"This is why Commander Pearson was so clued up when he came calling," said Tobi.

Chiaki carefully looked through all the file names on all the records that had popped up. She even opened up a few files and skimmed through them.

Her eyes became glossy as memories of her brother replayed in her mind.

There was one filename out of all of them that caught her eye.

Jonathan Flurick in Relaun

For this document to be showing up in the search results, it meant that her brother's name appeared somewhere within the document. Chiaki opened the file and began skim reading.

We thought that allowing Flurwick to assemble his own team to raid New Yoy would bring satisfying results, but little did we know that Flurwick carried the same genetics of the ancient galactic race that had birthed the Thundercloaks. Somehow the Thundercloaks realized this and this led to Flurwick abandoning his mission objectives.

"Serves you assholes right," Chiaki said. She continued reading.

After analyzing the data we recently secured from New Yoy, we can now fill in the gaps of what happened during

Flurwick's time there. It was a man known as Narbeth the Traveler that identified Flurwick as a descendant from Yoyvis— a planet erased from existence. Sometime after doing so, Narbeth told Flurwick about the lost powers of the Yoyvis people. These powers are considered magic abilities that could only be performed by the Elves and humans of Yoyvis. Narbeth claimed that these powers were casted away into a hidden realm called Relaun, and that the powers could be reclaimed should a descendant go back there and find the Celestibus.

Flurwick stayed on New Yoy for many days, ignoring all communications with the Alliance, and soon he'd made an agreement with Narbeth that he would use his resources as a marine to enter Relaun and reclaim the Celestibus. Flurwick had officially gone rogue and was working against the wishes of the Galactic Alliance.

But another individual on New Yoy went behind Narbeth's back.

Chiaki skipped a few paragraphs ahead, to avoid re-reading what she already knew. And then she read the passage that changed everything.

Flurwick now had conflicting thoughts on his trip to Relaun. On one hand he could follow Narbeth's plan and enter Relaun to reclaim the Celestibus and bring magic back to the Milky

Way, awakening magic inside all species with Yoyvis genes. Or, he could follow the new tip he'd been given and attempt to find the Death Shard that would allow him to absorb the Celestibus and become the only being in the Milky Way with the ability to use magic.

Without a doubt, there isn't a being alive who would resist the latter option. But Flurwick needed to know that there was truth to what he was being told. The Elf that tipped him off about the Death Shard had mentioned that there were ancient scrolls on Earth, and he was absolutely correct.

In Earth year nineteen-twenty-two some artifacts were discovered in Egypt, along with the discovery of of an ancient Egyptian tomb were artifacts with symbolism that matched nothing else discovered within Egypt. These were confiscated and locked away, staying hidden in a British museum for centuries.

It is not known how much knowledge Flurwick had on the scrolls' whereabouts, or what the scrolls showed, but we know trough Comm-link tracking that Flurwick visited planet Flade a number of times, seeking help from the hacker, Kura Nakayama, to locate and find these scrolls.

Chiaki's jaw dropped. "What?" She read through the next few sentences at an accelerated speed.

Each time Chiaki re-read that last sentence she stopped breathing, causing palpitations as tears streamed from her eyes. All this time, it was an Alliance marine that had claimed her brother's life. Not a gang, not a bounty hunter, or someone who'd been on the receiving end of a hack. It was the Alliance all along. Maybe it wasn't an order from the top brass, but it had been done at the hands of a marine. That was enough for Chiaki to blame the entire organization. Worst of all, the murder had been unwarranted. Jonathan Flurwick had wanted to prevent news of this mysterious scroll from getting out, but Kura would never have exposed a paying client, unless they'd given him reason to. The ruthlessness of it enraged her. Her bionic arm shook uncontrollably on the desk as she failed to control her nerves.

"Nova," came Tobi's voice. He may only be an A.I, but Tobi was programmed well enough to understand human emotions. He was aware that Chiaki was in a state of deep hurt, and he'd adjusted his voice so that it was slow and soft spoken as a result. "I know that this isn't easy to process, but if you keep reading, there's something you may wish to know. I'll let you get to it in your own time."

"Xièxiè," she sniffed. When she'd composed herself enough, she continued reading through the document. It went on about how Flurwick had recruited a unit of marines. The unit consisted of two twin brothers with the surname, Cunningham; and a promising young marine named Natalya Carrick that he respected. Flurwick then set up the entryway to Relaun on an uncharted world named Nurvoa. To achieve this, he'd used technology provided to him by Narbeth. It spoke about how Commander Pearson had learned of Flurwick's insubordination and had tried to prevent the news spreading throughout the organization.

Pearson had called for an operation that would have two marines enter Relaun to prevent Flurwick from succeeding and bringing chaos and disorder to the Milky Way. The Galactic Alliance feared not being able to regulate magical abilities, should Flurwick's or Narbeth's plans succeed. They opted not to tell the two marines the entire story, instead making them believe they were following up on the disappearances of their fellow marines. One of the marines, Brandon Wardson, had a medical condition and the other was a trouble maker with no real future in the Alliance. Pearson had figured that both men were expendable enough not to be missed for however long it took them to confront Flurwick—should they even succeed. Chiaki's arm continued to rock against the surface.

Eventually a gap in the document appeared, and below the gap was a new entry that had been added just three days ago.

The days we feared are among us now. Earlier today, Lieutenant-commander Jonathan Flurwick returned from Relaun. As suspected, he emerged on Nurvoa where he'd first entered the realm. With him, he had the Celestibus in a container and a solid piece of black crystal that we now know to be the Death Shard. Commander Pearson was standing by with the Lapwing. Flurwick was seen attempting to begin the procedure to absorb the Celestibus.

Seconds later, Natalya Carrick, Brandon Wardson and some beings who had existed within Relaun emerged from the same ripple that Flurwick had re-entered the Milky Way from. The two parties fought; with Natalya Carrick now appearing to be aligned with her ex-lover, Brandon Wardson. The Drekarth, which are the native species on Nurvoa also assisted in the fight.

It seemed Flurwick had the upperhand, exercising his new abilities, until Pearson's Lapwing descended from the sky. Flurwick was keen on avoiding any contact with the Galactic Alliance and decided to flee. In his haste, he left behind the Death Shard and one of Wardson's companions retrieved it.

As of now, we have opted to capture Brandon Wardson and his two companions from Relaun. They are currently being held in Trador as we cannot risk them interacting with any media outlets and blowing this story wide open before the Alliance has regained control. Separately, Natalya Carrick has agreed to co-operate and will work with the Alliance to locate Flurwick. Our objective as of now is to find Flurwick and make him see sense in working with us. With the Death Shard now in our possession, we have a bargaining chip with which to lure him. Commander Pearson has scheduled a meeting with top brass to discuss this matter, along with the fear of magic abilities that are now assumed to be awakening all over the Milky Way.

"What on Earth is going on right now?" said Chiaki with disbelief. The extent with which the Galactic Alliance wanted to control the Milky Way sickened her. They didn't care that a mad man with dangerous abilities was now on the loose, or that clueless Yoyvis descendants all over the Milky Way might be unknowingly waking up with new abilities. All that mattered to them was that they were in control, and not anyone else.

Chiaki pulled her arm away from the terminal, yanking the cable from it as a result. She slammed her synthetic fist through the screen, not really knowing why she was doing it. She was feeling and not thinking. "Flurwick and Pearson; they're both dead. I don't care how but I'm going to be the one to end them both."

"I'm not so sure about that," came a voice behind her.

Chiaki's stomach leaped up to her chest as she turned to face Vraxen.

CHAPTER FOURTEEN

"YOU!" CHIAKI YELLED. "Where the hell is he? Where is Pearson?" she glanced around the room as if he was hiding in the shadows.

"Pearson isn't here, Nova. But I am, because I've been tracking your ship since you left Flade."

In her rage, Chiaki hadn't processed that Vraxen was aiming a rifle at her. She pulled her SMG from her waist and aimed right back at him. "Why are you tracking me?"

"Pearson told me to keep an eye on you."

"Serious question, Vraxy; are you an idiot?" Through the window panes on the door behind Vraxen, Chiaki could see shadows indicating movement outside. A firefight was now a guarantee.

"You insult the one who saved your life?" Vraxen responded.

"I appreciate you keeping me alive and all, but if you're still siding with Pearson after he left you for dead then I'll happily accept you as the enemy. Your stupidity means you wouldn't make a good ally." His blue eyes widened. "I almost shot him for trying to leave without you, you know. I showed loyalty to you because you helped me. But now I guess it means nothing."

Behind Vraxen, two Alliance marines burst through the doors with their guns aimed in her direction. They stood either side of Vraxen. "Shoot her, now," one of the marines yelled. His voice was amplified through speakers on his helmet. "We have orders to shoot on sight."

"Hold on," said Vraxen, raising a hand from his laser rifle. "I've got this."

"We're giving it thirty seconds before we fire, merc."

"Come quietly," Vraxen said to her, "you'll keep your life if you follow my instruction."

Chiaki looked Vraxen dead in his eyes. "Pearson never paid that debt, Vraxen," she told him. "The loan sharks want you dead the moment you're seen on Utrion again."

Vraxen squinted his eyes, and she saw his chest inflate as he took a deep breath. The room became still and motionless to the point Chiaki could hear the moment one of the marines fingers squeezed over his trigger. Chiaki raised her synthetic arm in attempt to deflect the shot. She'd also turned her head sideways in fear; but in waiting for the impact she realized that no shot had made it her way. When she turned to look back at the marines, she saw that Vraxen had the shooter pinned against the door, wrestling the gun from his grip. The Stowyth had interrupted the marines shot and saved Chiaki.

The other marine was now pressing his gun to the side of Vraxen's head. "Stand down!" he yelled.

Galactic Alliance marine armor was modular, allowing each marine to mix and match pieces of armor to clip over their skinsuits. Both marines wore heavy armor plates on their upper body, but Chiaki noticed that in their haste, they'd not equipped leg pieces and were only wearing ordinary combat pants. Chiaki took advantage of this vulnerability by firing a shot at the marines' thigh. His screams echoed around the room as blood oozed through the hole in his pants. He crashed to his knees, wailing.

"You're lucky I don't use lasers, asshole." She

walked over to the marine who was now crouching down to comfort the wound and whipped her shiny new arm across his helmet, leaving a dent on the crown and knocking him out. Next to her, Vraxen was tossing the other marines' body across the room. His body crashed against the rack carrying the terminal; then, his body collided with the PVC floor tiles.

"We don't have long before the other marines come," said Vraxen. "We have to leave now."

Chiaki eyed him, half impressed at his decision to betray Pearson and half skeptical about whether he was double crossing her or not. After all the dirt she'd just read about the Alliance, she couldn't trust anyone. "How did you track me, Vraxy?"

"Pearson's unit left trackers on your ships when they held your people hostage. All I had to do was pay attention to where your ship was headed, after eight hours it was obvious to me that you were coming here."

"Tell me you have a shuttle waiting..." she said. With the station alerted to their presence, the odds of them staying alive long enough for her own shuttle to arrive was slim.

"It's on the roof, we just have to go out to the hall and take a ladder up. Follow me and put on your breather," he said. Chiaki was relieved.

✳ ✳ ✳

Chiaki followed Vraxen through the square panel at the top of the ladder. As her head emerged from the gap, Vraxen shot down a couple drones that were ready to spit a barrage of gunfire at them. When the threats were gone, Vraxen turned to help Chiaki up by the arm.

"This thing looks fancy, what else does it do?" he asked, tugging on her cold metal fingers.

Chiaki smirked as she pulled herself up. "It eliminates the need for men, if you know what I mean."

She could see a navy blue shuttle, parked thirty meters away. On the other side of the shuttle, a couple of marines landed on the roof using Jet Boosters. Immediately, Chiaki noticed one of them was of the Guaghul species.

Vraxen removed a compact weapon from his back holster and handed it to Chiaki. "Take this and shoot. An SMG won't cut it here. Just hit the button on the side to decompress it."

Chiaki held the front handle of the weapon firmly with her synthetic hand and followed Vraxen's instruction by tapping the button with her right hand. The weapon's nozzle extended from the front, and an extra handle popped out at the back. She raised the weapon to a comfortable position and took aim. The marines then took cover behind the shuttle.

"Cover me," said Vraxen. "I need to get in close and make sure they don't tamper with the shuttle."

Vraxen's legs extended, making him shoot up a couple feet taller. He used his extra height to sprint across the roof, covering a larger distance with each step.

Chiaki continued to move forward, aiming through the weapon's sights along the way. When she saw one of the marines pop up to take a shot, she fired at his shoulder and saw a bright red bolt fly through the air. There was no recoil. She wasn't sure if the shot had hit the marine, but he slipped out of sight without firing his own shot.

When Vraxen made it to the shuttle, he used his momentum to leap right over, landing right in front of the marines. A few shots were fired, but Vraxen was able to dodge them and kick the guns from their owners' grasp. Both marines stood to engage Vraxen in close combat. He wouldn't be able to keep this up too long, because having a fistfight with a Guaghul was like throwing your hardest punches at a brick wall.

The Guaghul were often referred to as *tanks* because they could give and take astounding levels of damage on the battlefield. They were stout beings, with long heads that often had several small horns aligned from their crown right down to their nose. Their faces were wide and brutish; and like all species in the Alliance, the Guaghul had its own custom fitted helmet that wouldn't fit other beings' measurements.

Chiaki picked up her pace and ran to the shuttle until she had enough momentum to leap on top. Being so short, she was inches away from tripping herself on the hood of the shuttle for not gaining enough height from the leap. She was able to use her arm to correct her balance and with her momentum sustained, she leaped onto the human marine; wrapping her synthetic arm around his neck and locking him into a hold. Her legs dangled at the marines' sides and he made desperate attempts to flip her off his back. Chiaki tensed and applied as much pressure around his neck as possible. The marine was leaning his chin down so that the cusp of his helmet would block her arm from tightening around his neck. Chiaki dug her right elbow into his shoulder several times, forcing his head to whip sideways and then she locked her other arm around his throat even tighter.

Eventually, the marine fell backwards and Chiaki gasped as her back slammed against the hard surface. She kept the pressure around the marines' neck until she was sure he was knocked out; and then she slowly released him and shuffled herself from underneath his body.

When she looked up, she saw that the Guaghul had wrestled Vraxen to the ground and had begun pummeling him with his three fingered fist. Chiaki got up close behind him and laced him with multiple kicks across his spine until he stopped beating Vraxen. When the Guaghul turned to face her, Chiaki immediately threw a fist to its helmet using her synthetic arm, but the Guaghul showed no sign of being affected. She hit him again, and then again, and then again; until the Guaghul blocked her and landed a haymaker to her chest—winding her.

The Guaghul was about to follow up on the attack, but Chiaki saw Vraxen's extended frame rise up behind the marine and lock him into a hold. "Time to take a page out of your book," said Vraxen, as he locked his arm around the marines' neck. When Chiaki had caught her breath she closed her synthetic palm into a fist and used her nerves to pop a small spike from the top of the knuckle. She slammed the fist into the Guaghul's abdomen.

"Tobi, shock him!" she yelled. And then an electroshock was released through her arm, leading right to the spike and into the marines' body. It was a custom mod that she'd built into the arm herself.

The Guaghul's body jerked for some time until it went limp, at which point Chiaki withdrew her fist.

When Vraxen released the marine, his body crashed against the giant roof tile. Chiaki felt she might pass out, as the electroshock left her spent.

"Are you alright?" asked Vraxen.

"I'll be fine in a minute, just get me in the shuttle," she said, walking to the vehicle, off balance.

Vraxen typed a code on the shuttle's security panel and it sprung to life. "Open up," he said. When the doors had opened he helped Chiaki into the shuttle and into her seat.

"So," said Vraxen, watching Chiaki from the opposite seat. They had removed their helmets and their breathers to get comfortable as the shuttle lifted them into the air.

"So," she said, still regaining her strength.

"What's the plan here? Are we going to your ship or mine? I parked a little further out than you."

"Is it an Alliance ship?" she asked.

"It was provided to me by Pearson, yes. But it's not an official vessel."

"What number FTL do you have?"

"Just a level two," he said. "I guess Pearson didn't want to spend a whole lot on me."

"We're taking mine then, and you're going to show me where the tracker is."

Vraxen opened a small compartment next to him and pulled a soda from it. He offered it to Chiaki. It was a glucose based energy drink. Chiaki didn't want to accept it, but she did because her body told her she needed it. She popped the spring and took a long sip from the can.

"Ahhh," she said with satisfaction.

"What's next then?" Vraxen asked. "I hope you have a plan, because Pearson won't take our newly established partnership lightly. He'll try to find us."

"Good, let the asshole come. He needs to be taught a lesson."

"You think you can take on an Alliance commander?"

"Not alone," she said, and she looked him in the eye.

"I might be good," he smirked, "but even I'm not egotistical enough to think that I alone can stand up to the Alliance marines."

"Then we fight fire with fire," said Chiaki, swaying the can of soda in her hand as she spoke. "We recruit our own Alliance marine."

Vraxen laughed. "And how do you expect to do that?"

Chiaki crossed her legs and took another sip of soda. She burped and felt her body kicking into gear again. "We're going to Trador, Vraxy."

"What? You want to go to the same prison that they want to lock us up in? You want us to turn ourselves in?"

"No way," she said. "We're going to spring out a marine they have locked up there. A guy called Brandon Wardson."

Chiaki watched Vraxen's eyes twitch and she was sure that it was the Stowyth equivalent of a roll of the eyes. "Well, I have no home to go to and I have no more work, so I guess I have no choice but to follow you." Vraxen shook his head. "From loan sharks, to marines, to hackers and weird people with pointy ears; how the hell did I get myself in this mess?"

Chiaki took a final swig of the soda and crushed

the can in her new hand. "Like my brother used to say, before a marine murdered him, sometimes you have no control over your path." And when she looked out of the window she saw the Yamata coming into view.

THE END

Chiaki (a.k.a Nova) will return in Realm Blender Book Two. Please read Realm Blender Book One if you haven't already.

About the Author

Gary Swaby is a writer who suffers from sickle cell anemia. After suffering from chronic pain all of his life, he gravitated towards video games, computers, books, anime, and comics.

Follow Gary on Twitter at: @GarySwaby and check out his blog **www.garyaswaby.com** for more info on sickle cell and his book projects.

www.garyaswaby.com

ACKNOWLEDGMENTS

This book is for all my fellow geeks, and otakus out here.

I have to thank my mum, Vanielee, for working hard all these years to ensure I always had a place to rest in my times of pain. Without her, I wouldn't have had the time or place to express my creativity.

Thanks to all my closest family members for supporting me through the years: Greg, Grandad, Kiesha and my Grandmother (Rest in peace).

These people have played an important part of my upbringing: Carmen, Michael, Robert, Colin, Oliver, Kieran Blackman, Anette, Shirley, Mark, Murray, Jenny, Masha, Aunty Daphne and Uncle Beanie, Kieran Todd, Kyle Ross, David, Una, Nicky, Lisa and everyone else who has been an important part of my life.

When I go through hard times, there are a few people that I consider to be my support system. We share the good and the bad with each other; and I can't go a day without the jokes these people provide; thanks a bunch: Carl Ebanks, Rameez Quadri, Richard Bailey, Edward Velazquez, Ilesha Knight, Dana Abercrombie, Tony Polanco, Anthony Frasier, James G, Fergus Mills, David Jagneaux, Tatjana and Torrence Davis.

Thanks to Garrett Glass for showing me everything that was wrong with my writing and helping me to slowly improve. I hope I didn't let you down.

I've spent countless hours of my life playing online video games with Clemens and Emma, and those games we play are some of my biggest inspirations. Thanks for the hours!

Thank you to Julienne for being the first to officially call me a writer. That's what gave me the confidence to begin putting this book together.

And thank you to the Sickle Cell Society.

Thanks for reading! Please add a short review and let me know what you thought!